THE JEMIMA SHORE MYSTERIES

Meet Jemima Shore: attractive and independent yet frequently thwarted in romance; a Protestant ex-convent girl; a successful TV reporter and a determined amateur sleuth. Despite her glamorous and absorbing career on TV Jemima has a habit of finding herself on the scene when a crime has been committed – and she also has a knack of hunting down the perpetrator. Whether she's on a remote Scottish island, in a quiet convent or visiting Oxford University, Jemima is sure to find herself in the middle of an intriguing mystery . . .

There are eight Jemima Shore mysteries to collect and two collections of short stories.

Since 1969, Antonia Fraser has written many acclaimed historical works which have been international bestsellers, as well as a mystery series featuring Jemima Shore. Her efforts in non-fiction have been awarded the James Tait Black Memorial Prize, the St Louis Literary Award, the CWA Non-Fiction Gold Dagger and the Wolfson Award for History. In 2000, she was awarded the Norton Medlicott Medal by the Historical Association and was made DBE in 2011 for her services to literature. She was married to Harold Pinter, who died on Christmas Eve 2008: her bestselling memoir of their life together *Must You Go?* was published in 2010. Her autobiography *My History: A Memoir of Growing Up* was published in 2015. Visit her website at www.antoniafraser.com.

Non-fiction by Antonia Fraser

Mary Queen of Scots
Cromwell: Our Chief of Men
King James VI of Scotland, I of England
King Charles II
The Weaker Vessel: Woman's Lot in Seventeenth-Century England
The Warrior Queens: Boadicea's Chariot
The Six Wives of Henry VIII
The Gunpowder Plot: Terror and Faith in 1605
Marie Antoinette: The Journey
Love and Louis XIV: The Women in the Life of the Sun King
Must You Go? My Life with Harold Pinter
Perilous Question
My History: A Memoir of Growing Up

Jemima Shore's First Case

and other stories

ANTONIA FRASER

WEIDENFELD & NICOLSON

For Emma Tennant
with love

A W&N PAPERBACK

First published in Great Britain in 1986
by George Weidenfeld & Nicolson Ltd
This edition published in 2015
by Weidenfeld & Nicolson,
an imprint of Orion Books Ltd,
Carmelite House, 50 Victoria Embankment,
London EC4Y 0DZ

An Hachette UK company

1 3 5 7 9 10 8 6 4 2

A CIP catalogue record for this book
is available from the British Library.

ISBN 978-1-7802-2862-4

Printed and bound in Great Britain
by Clays Ltd, St Ives plc

The Orion Publishing Group's policy is to use papers
that are natural, renewable and recyclable products and
made from wood grown in sustainable forests. The logging
and manufacturing processes are expected to conform to
the environmental regulations of the country of origin.

www.orionbooks.co.uk

Contents

Author's Note

The events in 'Jemima Shore's First Case' take place many years before those in *Quiet as a Nun*, the first full-length Jemima Shore mystery, but in the same setting and involving some of the same characters.

The other stories have appeared in magazines and anthologies including *The Anthology of Scottish Ghost Stories* (ed. Giles Gordon), *Cosmopolitan, John Creasey's Crime Collection* (ed. Herbert Harris), *Ellery Queen Mystery Magazine, The Fiction Magazine, Winter's Crimes, The Best of Winter's Crimes, Woman* Magazine, *Woman's Journal, Woman's Own* and the *Year's Best Mystery and Suspense Stories,* 1984 (edited by Edward D Hoch). To all the editors who chose or commissioned them, I am extremely grateful.

Jemima Shore's First Case

At the sound of the first scream, the girl in bed merely stirred and turned over. The second scream was much louder and the girl sat up abruptly, pushing back the meagre bedclothes. She was wearing a high-necked white cotton nightdress with long sleeves which was too big for her. The girl was thin, almost skinny, with long straight pale-red hair and oddly shaped slanting eyes in a narrow face.

Her name was Jemima Shore and she was fifteen years old.

The screams came again: by now they sounded quite blood-curdling to the girl alone in the small room – or was it that they were getting nearer? It was quite dark. Jemima Shore clambered out of bed and went to the window. She was tall, with long legs sticking out from below the billowing white cotton of the nightie, legs which like the rest of her body were too thin for beauty. Jemima pulled back the curtain which was made of some unlined flowered stuff. Between the curtain and the glass was an iron grille. She could not get out. Or, to put it another way, whatever was outside in the thick darkness, could not get in.

It was the sight of the iron grille which brought Jemima properly to her senses. She remembered at last exactly where she was: sleeping in a ground-floor room at a boarding-school

9

in Sussex called the Convent of the Blessed Eleanor. Normally Jemima was a day-girl at the Catholic boarding-school, an unusual situation which had developed when her mother came to live next door to Blessed Eleanor's in her father's absence abroad. The situation was unusual not only because Jemima was the only day-girl at Blessed Eleanor's but also because Jemima was theoretically at least a Protestant: not that Mrs Shore's vague ideas of religious upbringing really justified such a positive description.

Now Mrs Shore had been called abroad to nurse her husband who was recovering from a bad attack of jaundice, and Reverend Mother Ancilla, headmistress of the convent, had agreed to take Jemima as a temporary boarder. Hence the little ground-floor room – all that was free to house her – and hence for that matter the voluminous nightdress, Mrs Shore's ideas of nightclothes for her teenage daughter hardly according with the regulations at Blessed Eleanor's. To Jemima, still staring uncomprehendingly out into the darkness which lay beyond the grille and the glass, as though she might perceive the answer, none of this explained why she should now suddenly be awakened in the middle of the night by sounds which suggested someone was being murdered or at least badly beaten up: the last sounds you would expect to hear coming out of the tranquil silence which generally fell upon the Blessed Eleanor's after nine o'clock at night.

What *was* the time? It occurred to Jemima that her mother had left behind her own smart little travelling-clock as a solace in the long conventual nights. Squinting at its luminous hands – somehow she did not like to turn on the light and make herself visible through the flimsy curtains to whatever was outside in the night world – Jemima saw it was three o'clock. Jemima was not generally fearful either of solitude or the dark (perhaps because she was an only child) but the total indifference with which the whole convent appeared to be greeting the screams struck her as even more alarming than the noise itself. The big red-brick building, built in the twenties, housed not only a girls' boarding-school but the community of nuns who looked after them; the two areas were divided by the chapel.

The chapel! All of a sudden Jemima realized not only that the screams were coming from that direction but also – another sinister thought – she might conceivably be the only person within earshot. The so-called 'girls' guest-room' (generally old girls) was at the very edge of the lay part of the building. Although Jemima had naturally never visited the nuns' quarters on the other side, she had had the tiny windows of their cells pointed out by her best friend Rosabelle Powerstock, an authority on the whole fascinating subject of nuns. The windows were high up, far away from the chapel.

Was it from a sense of duty, or was it simply due to that ineradicable curiosity in her nature to which the nuns periodically drew grim attention suggesting it might be part of her unfortunate Protestant heritage . . . at all events, Jemima felt impelled to open her door a crack. She did so gingerly. There was a small night-light burning in the long corridor before the tall statue of the Foundress of the Order of the Tower of Ivory – Blessed Eleanor, dressed in the black habit the nuns still wore. The statue's arms were outstretched.

Jemima moved warily in the direction of the chapel. The screams had ceased but she did hear some other sound, much fainter, possibly the noise of crying. The night-light cast a dim illumination and once Jemima passed the statue with its long welcoming arms – welcoming, that is, in daylight; they now seemed to be trying to entrap her – Jemima found herself in virtual darkness.

As Jemima cautiously made her way in to the chapel, the lingering smell of incense began to fill her nostrils, lingering from that night's service of benediction, that morning's mass, and fifty other years of masses said to incense in the same place. She entered the chapel itself – the door was open – and perceived a few candles burning in front of a statue to her left. The incense smell was stronger. The little red sanctuary lamp seemed far away. Then Jemima stumbled over something soft and shapeless on the floor of the central aisle.

Jemima gave a sharp cry and at the same time the bundle moved, gave its own anguished shriek and said something which sounded like: 'Zeeazmoof, Zeeazmoof'. Then the bundle sat up and revealed itself to be not so much a bundle as an Italian girl in Jemima's own form called Sybilla.

At this point Jemima understood that what Sybilla was actually saying between sobs was: 'She 'as moved, she 'as moved', in her characteristic strong Italian accent. There was a total contrast between this sobbing creature and the daytime Sybilla, a plump and rather jolly dark-haired girl, who jangled in illicit gold chains and bracelets, and wore more than a hint of equally illicit make-up. Jemima did not know Sybilla particularly well despite sharing classes with her. She pretended to herself that this was because Sybilla (unlike Jemima and her friends) had no interest in art, literature, history or indeed anything very much except Sybilla herself; pleasure, parties and the sort of people you met at parties, principally male. Sybilla was also old for her form – seventeen already – whereas Jemima was young for it, so that there was a considerable age gap between them. But the truth was that Jemima avoided Sybilla because she was a princess (albeit an Italian one, not a genuine British Royal) and Jemima, being middle class and proud of it, had no wish to be accused of snobbery.

The discovery of Sybilla – Princess Maria Sybilla Magdalena Graffo di Santo Stefano to give her her full title – in the chapel only deepened the whole mystery. Knowing Sybilla, religious mania, a sudden insane desire to pray alone in the chapel at night, to make a novena for example, simply could not be the answer to her presence. Sybilla was unashamedly lazy where religion was concerned, having to be dragged out of bed to go to mass even when it was obligatory on Sundays and feast days, protesting plaintively, like a big black cat ejected from the fireside. She regarded the religious fervour of certain other girls, such as Jemima's friend Rosabelle Powerstock, with good-natured amazement.

'So boring' she was once overheard to say about the Feast of the Immaculate Conception (a holiday of obligation). 'Why do we have this thing? I think we don't have this thing in Italy.' It was fortunate that Sybilla's theological reflections on this occasion had never come to the ears of Reverend Mother Ancilla who would have quickly set to rights this unworthy descendant of a great Roman family (and even, delicious rumour said, of a Pope or two).

Yes, all in all, religious mania in Princess Sybilla could definitely be ruled out.

'Sybilla,' said Jemima, touching her shoulder, 'don't cry –'

At that moment came at last the sound for which Jemima had been subconsciously waiting since she first awoke: the characteristic swoosh of a nun in full habit advancing at high speed, rosary at her belt clicking, rubber heels twinkling down the marble corridor.

'Sybilla, *Jemima*?' The rising note of surprise on the last name was evident in the sharp but controlled voice of Sister Veronica, the Infirmarian. Then authority took over and within minutes nun-like phrases such as 'To bed at once both of you' and 'No more talking till you see Reverend Mother in the morning' had calmed Sybilla's convulsive sobs. The instinctive reaction of nuns in a crisis, Jemima had noted, was to treat teenage girls as children; or perhaps they always mentally treated them as children, it just came to the surface in a crisis. Sybilla after all was nearly grown-up, certainly if her physical appearance was any guide. Jemima sighed; was she to be hustled to bed with her curiosity, now quite rampant, unsatisfied?

It was fortunate for Jemima that before despatching her charges, Sister Veronica did at least make a quick inspection of the chapel - as though to see what other delinquent pupils might be lurking there in the middle of the night.

'What happened, Sybilla?' Jemima took the opportunity to whisper. 'What frightened you? I thought you were being murdered – '

Sybilla extended one smooth brown arm (unlike most of the girls at Blessed Eleanor's, she was perpetually sun-tanned, and unlike Jemima, she had somehow avoided wearing the regulation white nightdress).

'Oh, my God, Jemima!' It came out as 'Omigod, Geemima! I am telling you. She 'as moved!'

'Who moved, Sybilla?'

'The statue. You know, the one they call the Holy Nelly. She moved her arms towards me. She 'as touched me, Jemima. It was *miraculo*. How do you say? A mir-a-cul.'

Then Sister Veronica returned and imposed silence, silence on the whole subject.

But of course it was not to be like that. The next morning at assembly the whole upper school, Jemima realized, was buzzing with excitement in which words like 'miracle', 'Sybilla's miracle' and 'there was a miracle, did you hear' could be easily made out. Compared to the news of Sybilla's miracle – or the Blessed Eleanor's miracle depending on your point of view – the explanation of Sybilla's presence near the chapel in the middle of the night passed almost unnoticed: except by Jemima Shore that is, who definitely did not believe in miracles and was therefore still more avid to hear about Sybilla's experiences than she had been the night before. Jemima decided to tackle her just after Sister Hilary's maths lesson, an experience calculated to leave Sybilla unusually demoralized.

Sybilla smiled at Jemima, showing those dimples in her pinkish-olive cheeks which were her most attractive feature. (Come to think of it, was that pinkish glow due to a discreet application of blush-on? But Jemima, no nun, had other things on her mind.)

'Eet's ridiculous,' murmured Sybilla with a heavy sigh; there was a clank as her gold charm bracelet hit the desk; it struck Jemima that the nuns' rosaries and Sybilla's jewellery made roughly the same sound and served the same purpose, to advertise their presence. 'But you know these nuns, they won't let me write to my father. So boring. Oh yes, they will let me *write*, but it seems they must read the letter. Mamma made them do that, or maybe they did it, I don't know which.

Mamma is so holy, Omigod, she's like a nun . . . Papa' – Sybilla showed her dimples again – 'Papa, he is – how do you say – a bit of a bad dog.'

'A gay dog,' suggested Jemima helpfully. Sybilla ignored the interruption. She was busy speaking affectionately even yearningly of Prince Graffo di Santo Stefano's bad (or gay) dog-like tendencies which seemed to include pleasure in many different forms. (The Princess being apparently in contrast a model of austere piety, Jemima realized that Sybilla was very much her father's daughter.) The Prince's activities included racing in famous motor cars and escorting famously beautiful women and skiing down famous slopes and holidaying on famous yachts, and other things, amusing things. 'Papa he 'ates to be bored, he 'ates it!' These innocuous pursuits had according to Sybilla led the killjoy Princess to forbid her husband access to his daughter: this being Italy there could of course be no divorce either by the laws of the country or for that matter by the laws of Mother Church to which the Princess at least strictly adhered.

'But it's true, Papa, he doesn't want a divorce either,' admitted Sybilla. 'Then he might have to marry – I don't know who but he might have to marry this woman or that woman. That would be terrible for Papa. So boring. No, he just want some money, poor Papa, he has no money, Mamma has all the money, I think it's not fair that, she should *give* him the money, *si*, he is her *marito*, her 'usband, she should give it to him. What do you think, Jemima?'

Jemima, feeling the first stirrings of primitive feminism in her breast at this description of the Santo Stefano family circumstances, remained politely silent on that subject.

Instead: 'And the statue, Sybilla?' she probed gently.

'Ah.' Sybilla paused. 'Well, you see how it is, Jemima. I write to him. I write anything, amusing things. And I put them in a letter but I don't like the nuns to read these things so – ' she paused again. 'So I am making an arrangement with Gregory,' ended Sybilla with a slight but noticeable air of defiance.

'Yes, Gregory,' she repeated. 'That man. The gardener, the chauffeur, the odd-things man, whatever he is, the taxi-man.'

Jemima stared at her. She knew Gregory, the convent's new odd-job man, a surprisingly young fellow to be trusted in this all-female establishment, but all the same –

'And I am placing these letters under the statue of the Holy Nelly in the night,' continued Sybilla with more confidence. 'To wake up? Omigod, no problem. To go to sleep early, *that* is the problem. They make us go to bed like children here. And he, Gregory, is collecting them when he brings the post in the morning. Later he will leave me an answer which he takes from the post office. That day there will be one red flower in that big vase under the statue. And so we come to the night when I am having my *miraculo*,' she announced triumphantly.

But Jemima who did not believe in miracles, fell silent once more at what followed: Sybilla's vivid description of the statue's waving arms, warm touch just as she was about to hide the letter (which she then retrieved) and so forth and so on – an account which Jemima had a feeling was rapidly growing even as she told it.

'So you see I am flinging myself into the chapel,' concluded Sybilla. 'And sc-r-r-reaming and sc-r-r-reaming. Till you, Jemima *cara*, have found me. Because you only are near me!'

Well, that at least was true, thought Jemima: because she had formed the strong impression that Sybilla for all her warmth and confiding charm was not telling her the truth; or not the whole truth. Just as Jemima's reason would not let her believe in miracles, her instinct would not let her believe in Sybilla's story, at any rate not all of it.

Then both Jemima and Sybilla were swirled up in the sheer drama of Sister Elizabeth's lesson on her favourite Wordsworth ('Oh, the lovely man!').

'Once did she hold the gorgeous East in fee,' intoned Sister Liz in a sonorous voice before adding rather plaintively: 'Sybilla, do wake up; this is *your* Venice after all, as well as dear Wordsworth's.' Sybilla raised her head reluctantly from her desk where it had sunk as though under the weight of the thick dark hair, unconfined by any of the bands prescribed by convent rules. It was clear that her thoughts were very far from Venice, 'hers' or anyone else's, and even further from Wordsworth.

Another person who did not believe in miracles or at any rate did not believe in this particular miracle was Reverend Mother Ancilla. Whether or not she was convinced by Sybilla's explanation of sleep-walking – 'since a child I am doing it' – Mother Ancilla dismissed the mere idea of a moving statue.

'Nonsense child, you were asleep at the time. You've just said so. You dreamt the whole thing. No more talk of miracles please, Sybilla; the ways of Our Lord and indeed of the Blessed Eleanor may be mysterious but they are not as mysterious as *that*,' announced Mother Ancilla firmly with the air of one to whom they were not in fact at all that mysterious in the first place. 'Early nights for the next fourteen days – no, Sybilla, that is what I said, you need proper rest for your mind which is clearly, contrary to the impression given by your report, over-active . . .'

Even Sybilla dared do no more than look sulky-faced with Mother Ancilla in such a mood. The school as a whole was compelled to take its cue from Sybilla: with no further grist to add to the mill of gossip, gradually talk of Sybilla's miracle died away to be replaced by scandals such as the non-election of the Clitheroe twins Annie and Pettie (short for Annunziata and Perpetua) as Children of Mary. This was on the highly unfair grounds that they had appeared in a glossy magazine in a series called 'Cloistered Moppets' wearing some Mary Quantish version of a nun's habit.

Jemima Shore did sometimes wonder whether Sybilla's illicit correspondence still continued. She also gazed from time to time at Gregory as he went about his tasks, all those tasks which could not be performed by the nuns themselves (surprisingly few of them as a matter of fact, picking up and delivering the post being one of them). Gregory was a solid-looking individual in his thirties with nice thick curly hair cut quite short, but otherwise in no way striking; were he not the only man around the convent grounds (with the exception of visiting priests in the morning and evening and parents at weekends) Jemima doubted whether she would have remembered his face. But he was a perfectly pleasant person, if not disposed to chat, not to Jemima Shore at least. The real wonder was, thought Jemima, that Sybilla had managed to corrupt him in the first place.

It was Jemima's turn to sigh. She had better face facts. Sybilla was rich – that much was obvious from her appearance – and she was also voluptuous. Another sigh from Jemima at the thought of Sybilla's figure, so much more like that of an Italian film star – if one fed on dollops of spaghetti – than anything Jemima could achieve. No doubt both factors, money and figure, had played their part in enabling Sybilla to capture Gregory. It was time to concentrate on other things – winning the English Prize for example (which meant beating Rosabelle) or securing the part of Hamlet in the school play (which meant beating everybody).

When Sybilla appeared at benediction on Saturday escorted by a middle-aged woman, and a couple of men in camel-haired coats, one very tall and dark, the other merely dark, Jemima did spare some further thought for the Santo Stefano family. Were these relations? The convent rules were strict enough for it to be unlikely they were mere friends, especially when Mamma Principessa was keeping such a strict eye on access to her daughter. Besides, the woman did bear a certain resemblance to Sybilla, her heavily busted figure suggesting how Sybilla's voluptuous curves might develop in middle age.

Jemima's curiosity was satisfied with unexpected speed: immediately after benediction Sybilla waved in her direction, and with wreathed smiles and much display of dimple, introduced her cousin Tancredi, her Aunt Cristiana and her Uncle Umberto.

'Ah now, Jemima, you come with us, yes, you come with us for dinner? Yes, I insist. You have saved me. *Si, si*, it was her' – to her relations. To Jemima she confided: 'What a surprise, they are here. I am not expecting them. They come to spy on the naughty Sybilla,' dimples again. 'But listen, Tancredi, he is very much like my Papa, now you know what Papa looks like, 'andsome, yes? And Papa, he like Tancredi very much, so you come?'

'I don't have a Permission –' began Jemima rather desperately. One look at Tancredi had already told her that he approximated only too wonderfully to her latest ideal of masculine attraction, derived partly from the portrait of Lord Byron at the front of her O-level text, and partly from a character in a Georgette Heyer novel called *Devil's Cub*. (Like many would-be intellectuals, Jemima had a secret passion for Georgette Heyer. Jemima, with Rosabelle, Annie, Pettie and the rest of her coterie, were relieved when from time to time some older indisputably intellectual female would announce publicly in print, tribute perhaps to her own youth, that Georgette Heyer was an important if neglected literary phenomenon.)

Alas, Jemima felt in no way ready to encounter Tancredi, the man of her dreams, at this precise juncture: she was aware that her hair, her best feature, hung lankly, there having been no particular reason in recent days to wash it. Her 'home clothes' in which she would be allowed to emerge from the convent, belonged to a much shorter girl (the girl Mrs Shore had in fact bought the clothes for, twelve months previously), nor could they be passed off as mini-skirted because they were too unfashionable.

One way and another, Jemima was torn between excitement and apprehension when Sybilla, in her most wayward mood, somehow overrode these very real difficulties ('But it's charming, the long English legs; Tancredi has seen you, *ma che bella*! Yes, yes, I am telling you . . .') and also, even more surprisingly, convinced Mother Ancilla to grant permission.

'An unusual friendship, dear Jemima,' commented the Reverend Mother drily, before adding: 'But perhaps you and

Sybilla have both something to learn from each other.' Her bright shrewd little eyes beneath the white wimple moved down Jemima's blouse and that short distance covered by her skirt.

'Is that a mini-skirt?' asked Mother Ancilla sharply. 'No, no, I see it is not. And your dear mother away . . .' Mother Ancilla's thoughts were clearly clicking rapidly like the beads of her rosary. 'What will the Marchesa think? Now, child, go immediately to Sister Baptist in the sewing-room, I have a feeling that Cecilia Clitheroe' – she mentioned the name of a recent postulant, some relation to Annie and Pettie – 'is about your size.' Marvelling, not for the first time at the sheer practical worldliness of so-called unworldly nuns, Jemima found herself wearing not so much a drooping blouse and outmoded skirt as a black suit trimmed in beige braid which looked as if it had come from Chanel or thereabouts.

Without the suit, would Jemima really have captured Tancredi in quite the way she did at the dinner which followed? For undoubtedly, as Jemima related it to Rosabelle afterwards, Tancredi *was* captured and Rosabelle, summing up all the evidence agreed that it must have been so. Otherwise why the slow burning looks from those dark eyes, the wine glass held in her direction, even on one occasion a gentle pressure of a knee elegantly clad in a silk suit of a particular shade of blue just a little too bright to be English? As for Tancredi himself, was he not well worth capturing, the muscular figure beneath the dandyish suit, nothing effeminate about Tancredi, the atmosphere he carried with him of international sophistication – or was it just the delicious smell of *Eau Sauvage*? (Jemima knew it was *Eau Sauvage* because on Rosabelle's recommendation she had given some to her father for Christmas; not that she had smelt it on him subsequently beyond one glorious whiff at Christmas dinner itself.)

As for Sybilla's uncle and aunt, the Marchesa spoke very little but when she did so it was in careful English, delivered, whether intentionally or not, in a reproachful tone as though Jemima's presence at dinner demanded constant explanation if not apology. Jemima's answers to the Marchesa's enquiries about her background and previous education seemed to disgust her particularly; at one point, hearing that Jemima's father was serving in the British army, the Marchesa simply stared at her. Jemima hoped that the stare was due to national prejudice based on wartime memories, but feared it was due to simple snobbery.

Uncle Umberto was even quieter, a short pock-marked Italian who would have been plausible as a waiter, had he not been an Italian nobleman. Both uncle and aunt, after the first unfortunate interrogation, spoke mainly in Italian to their niece: family business, Jemima assumed, leaving Tancredi free for his pursuit of Jemima while their attention was distracted.

The next day: 'You 'ave made a conquest, Jemima' related Sybilla proudly. 'Tancredi finds you so int-ell-igent' – she drawled out the word – 'and he asks if all English girls are so int-ell-igent, but I say that you are famous for being clever, so clever that you must find him so stu-pid!'

'I'm not all *that* clever, Sybilla.' Jemima despite herself was nettled; for once she had hoped her attraction lay elsewhere than in her famous intelligence. That might win her the English Prize (she had just defeated Rosabelle) but intelligent was not quite how she wished to be regarded in those sophisticated international circles in which in her secret day-dreams she was now dwelling . . .

Tancredi's letter, when it came, did not however dwell upon Jemima's intelligence but more of her particular brand of English beauty, her strawberries-and-cream complexion (Sybilla's blush-on had been liberally applied), her hair the colour of Italian sunshine and so forth and so on in a way that Jemima had to admit could scarcely be bettered even in day-dream. The method by which the letter arrived was less satisfactory: the hand of Sybilla, who said that it had been enclosed in a letter from Tancredi's sister Maria Gloria (letters from accredited female relations were not generally opened). Had Sybilla read the letter which arrived sealed with sellotape?

If she had, Jemima was torn between embarrassment and pride at the nature of the contents.

Several more letters followed until one day – 'He wants to see you again. Of course he wants to see you again!' exclaimed Sybilla. 'He loves you. Doesn't he say so always?' Jemima shot her a look: so Sybilla did know the letters' contents. To her surprise Jemima found that she was not exactly eager to see Tancredi again, despite the fact that his smuggled letters had become the centre of her emotional existence. Tancredi's passion for Jemima had something of the miraculous about it – Jemima smiled to herself wryly, she who did not believe in miracles – and she couldn't help being worried that the miracle might not happen a second time . . . It was in the end more sheer curiosity than sheer romance which made Jemima continue to discuss Sybilla's daring idea for a rendezvous. This was to be in Jemima's own ground-floor room no less – Tancredi to be admitted through the grille left open for the occasion.

'The key!' cried Jemima 'No, it's impossible. How would we ever get the key?'

'Oh Jemima, you who are so clever,' purred Sybilla, looking more than ever like a fat black cat denied its bowl of cream. 'Lovely Jemima . . . I know you will be thinking of something. Otherwise I am thinking that Tancredi goes to Italy and you are not seeing him. So boring. He has so many girls there.'

'Like Papa?' Jemima could not resist asking. But Sybilla merely pouted.

'I could give such a long, long letter to Papa if you say yes,' she sighed. 'I'm frightened to speak to Gregory now, you know. Papa thinks –' She paused. 'He's a bit frightened. And I'm frightened too. That moving statue.' Sybilla shuddered.

'No, Sybilla,' said Jemima.

Nevertheless in her languorously persistent way, Sybilla refused to let the subject of Tancredi's projected daring expedition to Blessed Eleanor's drop. Jemima for her part was torn between a conviction that it was quite impossible to secure the key to the grille in front of her ground-floor window and a pride which made her reluctant to admit defeat, defeat at the hands of the nuns. In the end pride won, as perhaps Jemima had known all along that it would. She found by observing Sister Dympna, who swept her room and was responsible for locking the grille at darkness, that the grille was opened by a key, but snapped shut of its own accord. From there it was a small step to trying an experiment: a piece of blackened cardboard between grille and jamb, and the attention of Sister Dympna distracted at the exact moment the busy little nun was slamming the grille shut.

It worked. Jemima herself had to close the grille properly after Sister Dympna left. That night Jemima lay awake, conscious of the outer darkness and the window through which Tancredi would come if she wanted him to come. She began to review the whole thrilling affair, beginning so unpropitiously as it had seemed at the time, with Sybilla's screams in the night. She remembered that night in the chapel with the terrified girl, the smell of incense in her nostrils, and then switched her thoughts to her first and so far her only encounter with Tancredi . . . Her own personal miracle. She heard Sybilla's voice : '*Miraculo.*'

But I don't believe in miracles, said the coldly reasonable voice of Jemima enclosed in the darkness, away from the seductive Mediterranean charm of Sybilla. And there's something else too: my instinct. I thought she was lying that first night, didn't I? Why did the statue move? A further disquieting thought struck Jemima. She got out of bed, switched on the light, and gazed steadily at her reflection in the small mirror over the basin.

'Saturday,' said Jemima the next morning; she sounded quite cold. 'Maria Gloria had better pass the message.' But Sybilla, in her pleasure at having her own way, did not seem to notice the coldness. 'And Sybilla —' added Jemima.

'Cara?'

'Give me the letter for your father in good time because I've got permission to go over to my own house to borrow some decent dresses of my mother's, she's coming back, you know. As I may not see you later, give me the letter before I go.' Sybilla enfolded Jemima in a soft, warm, highly scented embrace.

By Saturday, Jemima found herself torn between two exactly contradictory feelings. Half of her longed for the night, for the rendezvous – whatever it might bring – and the other half wished that darkness would never come, that she could remain for the rest of her life, suspended, just waiting for Tancredi . . . Was this what being in love meant? For Jemima, apart from one or two holiday passions, for her father's young subalterns, considered that she had never been properly in love; although it was a matter much discussed between herself and Rosabelle (of her other friends the Clitheroe twins, Annie and Pettie being too merrily wanton and Bridget too strictly pious to join in these talks). Then there was another quite different side to her character, the cool and rational side, which simply said: I want to investigate, I want to find out what's going on, however painful the answer.

Jemima made her visit to her parents' home driven by the silent Gregory and chaperoned by Sister Veronica who was cross enough at the waste of time to agree with Jemima that the garden was in an awful state, and rush angrily at the neglected branches – 'Come along, Jemima, we'll do it together.' Jemima took a fork to the equally neglected beds and dug diligently out of range of Sister Veronica's conversation. (Gregory made no move to help but sat in the car.) Jemima herself was also extremely quiet on the way back, which with Gregory's enigmatic silence, meant that Sister Veronica could chatter on regarding the unkempt state of the Shore home ('Your poor dear mother . . . no gardener') to her heart's content. For the rest of the day and evening, Jemima had to keep the investigative side of her nature firmly to the fore. She found her emotional longings too painful.

Darkness fell on the convent. From the corner of her window – unbarred or rather with a crack left in the grille, so that only someone who knew it would open, would be able to detect it – Jemima could watch as the yellow lights in the high dormitories were gradually extinguished. Sybilla was sleeping somewhere up there in the room which she shared with a monkey-like French girl called Elaine, who even in the summer at Blessed Eleanor's was huddled against the cold: 'She is too cold to wake up. She is like your little mouse who sleeps,' Sybilla had told Jemima. But Sybilla now was certainly watched at night and could not move about freely as she had once done.

On the other side of the building were the nuns, except for those on duty in the dormitories or Sister Veronica in the infirmary. Jemima had no idea where Mother Ancilla slept – alone perhaps in the brief night allowed to nuns before the early morning mass? But Mother Ancilla was another subject about which Jemima preferred not to think; the nun was so famously percipient that it had required some mental daring for Jemima even to say goodnight to her. She feared that the dark shrewd eyes might see right through to her intentions.

In her room, Jemima decided not to change into her convent night gown; she snuggled under the covers in jeans (collected that afternoon from home – strictly not allowed at Blessed Eleanor's) – and a skimpy black polo-necked jersey. In spite of herself, convent habits inspired in her a surprising desire to pray.

Reflecting that to do so even by rationalist standards, could not exactly do any *harm*, Jemima said three Hail Marys.

Oddly enough it was not until Jemima heard the faint – very faint – sound of someone rapping on the window, which was her clue to wind back the grille, that it occurred to Jemima that what she was doing might not only be foolhardy but actively dangerous. By then of course it was too late. She had no course now but to pull back the grille as silently as possible – since Sybilla's escapade the nuns had taken to patrolling the outside corridor from time to time. She raised the window cautiously.

Over the sill, dressed as far as she could make out entirely in black, at any rate in black jersey (remarkably similar to her own) and black trousers, with black rubber-soled shoes, came

Tancredi. The smell of *Eau Sauvage* filled the room: for one wild moment the sweetness of it made Jemima regret . . . then she allowed herself to be caught into Tancredi's arms. He kissed her, his rather thin lips forcing apart her own.

Then Tancredi stood back a little and patted her lightly on her denim-clad thigh, 'What protection! You are certainly not anxious to seduce me, *cara*,' he said softly. Jemima could sense him smiling in the darkness. 'This is a little bit like a nun, yes?' He touched her breast in the tight black jersey. 'This not so much.'

'Tancredi, you mustn't, I mean –' What did she mean? She knew what she meant. She had it all planned, didn't she?

'Tancredi, listen, you've simply got to take Sybilla's packet, her letter that is, it's quite thick, the letter, you must take it and then go. You see, the nuns are very suspicious. I couldn't let you know, but I have a feeling someone suspects . . . Mother Ancilla, she's the headmistress, she's awfully beady.' Jemima was conscious she was babbling on. 'So you must take the letter and *go*.'

'Yes, I will take the letter. In good time. Or now, *tesoro*, if you like. I don't want to make tr-r-rouble for you.' Tancredi sounded puzzled. 'But first, oh I'm so tired, all that walking through this park, its enor-mous, let's sit down a moment on this ridiculous little bed. Now this is really for a nun, this bed.'

'I think you should just collect the letter and go,' replied Jemima, hoping that her voice did not quaver.

'Collect, you mean you don't have it' Trancredi was now a little brisker, more formal.

'I – I hid it. By the statue outside. You see we have inspection on Saturdays, drawer inspection, cupboard inspection, everything. I didn't dare keep it. So I used her place, Sybilla's place. Look, I'll explain where you go –'

To Jemima's relief, yes, it really was to her relief, she found Tancredi seemed to accept the necessity for speed, and even for a speedy departure. The embrace he gave her as he vanished into the ill-lit corridor was quite perfunctory, only the lingering smell of *Eau Sauvage* in her room reminded her of

what a romantic tryst this might under other circumstances
have turned out to be. Jemima sat down on the bed suddenly
and waited for Tancredi's return. Then there would be one last
embrace, perhaps perfunctory, perhaps a little longer, and he
would vanish into the darkness from which he had come, out
of her life.

She waited.

But things did not turn out quite as Jemima had planned.
One moment Tancredi was standing at the door again, with a
clear view of the big statue behind him; he had a pencil torch in
his hand and a packet opened at one end. The next moment he
had leapt towards her and caught her throat in the fingers of
one strongly muscled hand.

'Where is it?' he was saying in a fierce whisper, 'Where is it?
Have you taken it? Who has taken it?' And then, with more
indignation – 'What is *this*?' He was looking at some white
Kleenex which protruded from the packet, clearly addressed
to the Principe Graffo di Santo Stefano in Sybilla's flowing
hand. The fingers tightened on Jemima's throat so that she
could hardly speak, even if she had some answer to the fierce
questioning.

'Tancredi, I don't know what – ' she began. Then beyond
Tancredi, at the end of the corridor, to Jemima's horror she
saw something which looked to her very much like the statue
of the Blessed Eleanor moving. Jemima gave a scream, cut off
by the pressure of Tancredi's fingers. After that a lot of things
happened at once, so that later, sorting them out for Rosabelle
(under very strict oath of secrecy - the Clitheroe twins and
Bridget definitely not to be informed) Jemima found it
difficult to get the exact order straight. At one moment the
statue appeared to be moving in their direction, the next
moment a big flashlight, of quite a different calibre from
Tancredi's pencil torch, was shining directly on both of them.
It must have been then that Jemima heard the voice of
Gregory, except that Gregory was saying something like:
Detective Inspector Michael Vann, Drugs Squad, and Michael

Vann of the Drugs Squad was, it seemed, in the process of arresting Tancredi.

Or rather he might have intended to be in the process, but an instant after Tancredi heard his voice and was bathed in the flashlight, he abandoned his hold on Jemima, dived in the direction of the window, pulled back the grille and vanished.

Then there were more voices, an extraordinary amount of voices for a tranquil convent at night, and phrases were heard like 'Never mind, we'll get him', and words like 'Ports, airports', all of which reverberated in the mind of Jemima without making a particularly intelligible pattern. Nothing seemed to be making much sense, not since the statue had begun to move, until she heard someone – Gregory – say:

'And after all that, he's managed to take the stuff with him.'

'He hasn't,' said Jemima Shore in a small but firm voice. 'It's buried in the garden at home.'

It was so typical of Mother Ancilla, observed Jemima to Rosabelle when the reverberations of that night had at long last begun to die away, so typical of her that the very first thing she should say was: 'You're wearing jeans, Jemima.'

'I suppose she had to start somewhere,' commented Rosabelle. 'Personally, I think it's a bit much having the Drugs Squad moseying round the convent even if it is the biggest haul etc. etc. and even if the Principe is a wicked drug pusher etc. etc. Thank goodness it's all over in time for the school play.' Rosabelle had recently been cast as Hamlet (Jemima was cast as Laertes – 'that dear misguided *reckless* young man, as Sister Elizabeth put it, with a meaning look in Jemima's direction). Rosabelle at least had the school play much on her mind. 'Did Mother Ancilla give any proper explanation?' Rosabelle went on.

'You know Mother Ancilla,' Jemima said ruefully, 'She was really amazingly lofty about the whole thing. That is, until I remarked in a most innocent voice that the nuns obviously agreed with the Jesuits that the ends justify the means.'

'Daring! Then what?'

'Then I was told to write an essay on the history of the Society of Jesus by Friday – you can't win with Mother Ancilla.'

'Sybilla and Co. certainly didn't. Still, all things considered, you were quite lucky, Jem. You did save the cocaine. You didn't get struck down by Tancredi, and you didn't get ravished by him.'

'Yes, I was lucky; wasn't I?' replied Jemima in a tone in which Rosabelle thought she detected just a hint of wistfulness.

The reverberations of that night had by this time included the precipitate departure of Sybilla from the convent, vast amounts of expensive green velvety luggage surrounding her weeping figure in the convent hall the next day. She refused to speak to Jemima beyond spitting at her briefly: 'I *'ate* you, Jemima, and Tancredi, he 'ates you too, he thinks you are *ugly*.' Then Sybilla shook her black head furiously so that the long glittering earrings, which she now openly flaunted, jangled and glinted.

What would happen to Sybilla? The Drugs Squad were inclined to be lenient towards someone who was so evidently under the influence of a father who was both pleasure-loving and poverty-stricken (a bad combination). Besides, thanks to a tip-off, they had had her watched since her arrival in England, and the Prince's foolproof method of bringing drugs into the country via his daughter's school luggage – clearly labelled 'Blessed Eleanor's Convent, Churne, Sussex' – had never in fact been as foolproof as he imagined. For that matter Gregory, the enigmatic gardener, had not been as subornable as Sybilla in her confident way and Jemima in her envious one, had imagined.

Gregory however, as an undercover operative, had not been absolutely perfect; it had been a mistake for example to let Sybilla glimpse him that night by the statue, provoking that fit of hysterics which had the effect of involving Jemima in the whole affair. Although it could be argued – and was by Jemima and Rosabelle – that it was Jemima's involvement which had flushed out Tancredi, the Prince's deputy, after Sybilla had become too frightened to contact Gregory. Then there was Jemima's valiant entrapment of Tancredi and her resourceful preservation of the cocaine.

All the same, Jemima Shore herself had not been absolutely perfect in the handling of the whole matter, as Mother Ancilla pointed out very firmly, once the matter of the jeans had been dealt with. It was only after some very frank things had been said about girls who kept things to themselves, things best confided to authority, girls who contemplated late-night trysts with males (albeit with the highest motives as Mother Ancilla accepted) that Mother Ancilla put her bird's head on one side: 'But, Jemima dear child, what made you – how did you guess?'

'I just never believed in the second miracle, Mother,' confessed Jemima.

'The second miracle, dear child?'

'I didn't believe in the first miracle either, the miracle of Sybilla's waving statue. The second miracle was Tancredi, the cousin, falling in love with me. I looked in the mirror, and well . . .' Her voice tailed away. Mother Ancilla had the effect of making her confess things she would rather, with hindsight, have kept to herself.

Mother Ancilla regarded Jemima for a moment. Her gaze was quizzical but not unkind.

'Now Jemima, I am sure that when we have finished with you, you will make a wonder Ca– . . . a wonderful wife and mother' – she had clearly intended to say 'Catholic wife and mother' before realizing who sat before her.

Jemima Shore saw her first and doubtless her last chance to score over Mother Ancilla.

'Oh, no, Reverend Mother,' she answered boldly, 'I'm not going to be a wife and mother. I'm going into television,' and having already mentioned one of Mother Ancilla's pet banes, she was inspired to add another: 'I'm going to be an investigative reporter.'

The Case Of The Parr Children

'I've come about the children.'

The woman who stood outside the door of the flat, her finger poised to ring the bell again, looked desperate. She also looked quite unknown to the owner of the flat, Jemima Shore. It was ten o'clock on Sunday morning; an odd time for anyone to be paying a social call on the celebrated television reporter. Jemima Shore had no children. Outside her work she led a very free and very private existence. As she stood at the door, unusually dishevelled, pulling a dark-blue towelling robe round her, she had time to wonder rather dazedly: Whose children? Why here? Before she decided that the stranger had rung the wrong bell of the flat, and very likely in the wrong house in Holland Park.

'I've come about the children.'

The woman before her was panting slightly as she repeated the words. But then Jemima Shore's flat was on the top floor. It was her appearance which on closer inspection was odd: she looked smudged and dirty like a charcoal drawing which has been abandoned. Her beltless mackintosh had presumably once been white; as had perhaps her ancient tennis shoes with their gaping canvas, and her thick woollen socks. The thin dark dress she wore beneath her mackintosh, hem hanging down, gave the impression of being too old for her until Jemima realized that it was the dress itself which was decrepit. Only her hair showed any sign of care: that had at least been brushed. Short and brown, it hung down straight on either side of her face: in this case the style was too young.

The woman before Jemima might have been a tramp. Then there was the clink of a bottle at her feet as she moved uneasily towards Jemima. In a brown paper bag were the remains of a picnic which had clearly been predominantly alcoholic. The image of the tramp was confirmed.

'Jemima Shore Investigator?' she gasped. 'You've *got* to help me.' And she repeated for the third time: 'You see, I've come about the children.'

Jemima recoiled slightly. It was true that she was billed by this title in her programmes of serious social reportage. It was also true that the general public had from time to time mistaken her for a real investigator as a result. Furthermore, lured by the magic spell of know-all television, people had on occasion brought her problems to solve; and she had on occasions solved them. Nevertheless early on a Sunday morning, well before the first cup of coffee, seemed an inauspicious moment for such an appeal. In any case by the sound of it, the woman needed a professional social worker rather than an amateur investigator.

Jemima decided that the lack of coffee could at least be remedied. Pulling her robe still further around her, and feeling more than slightly cross, she led the way into her elegant little kitchen. The effect of the delicate pink formica surfaces was to make the tramp-woman look grubbier than ever. At which point her visitor leant forward on her kitchen stool, covered in pretty rose-coloured denim, and started to sob loudly and uncontrolledly into her hands. Tears trickled between her fingers. Jemima noticed with distaste that the finger-nails too were dirty. Coffee was by now not so much desirable as essential. Jemima proceeded first to make it, and then to administer it.

Ten minutes later she found herself listening to a very

strange story indeed. The woman who was telling it described herself as Mrs Catharine Parr.

'Yes, just like the wretched Queen who lost her head, and I'm just as wretched, I'm quite lost too.' Jemima raised her eyebrows briefly at the historical inaccuracy – hadn't Catharine Parr, sixth wife of Henry VIII, died in her bed? But as Mrs Parr rushed on with her dramatic tale, she reflected that here was a woman who probably embellished everything with unnecessary flourishes. Mrs Parr was certainly wretched enough; that went without question. Scotland. She had come overnight from Scotland. Hence of course the mackintosh, even the picnic (although the empty wine bottles remained unexplained). Hence the early hour, for Mrs Parr had come straight from Euston Station, off her sleeper. And now it was back to the children again.

At this point, Jemima Shore managed at last to get a word in edgeways: 'Whose children? Your children?'

Mrs Parr, tears checked, looked at Jemima as though she must already know the answer to that question: 'Why, the *Parr* children of course. Don't you remember the case of the Parr children? There was a lot about it on television,' she added reproachfully.

'The Parr children: yes, I think I do remember something – your children, I suppose.'

To Jemima's surprise there was a pause. Then Mrs Parr said with great solemnity:

'Miss Shore, that's just what I want you to find out. I just don't *know* whether they're my children or not. I just don't *know*.'

'I think,' said Jemima Shore Investigator, resignedly drinking her third cup of coffee, 'you had better tell me all about it from the beginning.'

Oddly enough Jemima genuinely did remember something about the episode. Not from television, but from the newspapers where it had been much discussed, notably in the *Guardian*; and Jemima was a *Guardian* reader. It had been a peculiarly rancorous divorce case. The elderly judge had come down heavily on the side of the father. Not only had he taken the unusual step of awarding Mr Parr care and custody of the two children of the marriage – mere babies – but he had also summed up the case in full for the benefit of the Press.

In particular he had dwelt venomously on the imperfections of Mrs Parr and her 'trendy amoral Bohemianism unsuitable for contact with any young creature'. This was because Mrs Parr had admitted having an affair with a gypsy or something equally exotic. She now proposed to take her children off with him for the glorious life of the open road; which, she suggested, would enable her children to grow up uninhibited, loving human beings. Mr Parr responded with a solid bourgeois proposition, including a highly responsible Nanny, a general atmosphere of nursery tea now, private schools later. Columnists had had a field-day for a week or two, discussing the relative merits of bourgeois and Bohemian life-styles for children. On the whole Jemima herself had sympathized with the warm-blooded Mrs Parr.

It transpired that Jemima's recollection of the case was substantially correct. Except that she had forgotten the crucial role played by the so-called Nanny; in fact no Nanny but a kind of poor relation, a trained nurse named Zillah. It was Zillah who had spoken with calm assurance of the father's love for his children, reluctantly of the selfish flightiness of the mother. She had known her cousin Catharine all her life, she said, although their material circumstances had been very different. She pronounced with regret that in her opinion Catharine Parr was simply not fitted to have sole responsibility for young children. It was one of the reasons which had prompted her to leave her nursing career in order to look after the Parr babies.

Since Zillah was clearly a detached witness who had the welfare of the children at heart, her evidence was regarded as crucial by the judge. He contrasted Catharine and Zillah: 'two young women so outwardly alike, so inwardly different'. He made this also a feature of his summing-up. 'Miss Zillah Roberts, who has had none of the benefits of money and education of the mother in the case, has nevertheless demonstrated the kind of firm moral character most appropriate to the care of infants . . . etc. etc.'

In vain Mrs Parr had exploded in court: 'Don't believe her! She's his mistress! They're sleeping together. She's been jealous of me all her life. She always wanted everything I had, my husband, now my children.' Such wild unsubstantiated talk did Mrs Parr no good at all, especially in view of her own admitted 'uninhibited and loving' behaviour. If anything, the judge's summing-up gained in vinegar from the interruption.

Mrs Parr skated over the next part of her story. Deprived of her children, she had set off for the south of Ireland with her lover. Jemima had the impression, listening to her, that drink had played a considerable part in the story – drink and perhaps despair too. Nor did Mrs Parr enlarge on the death of her lover, except to say that he had died as he had lived: 'violently'. As a result Jemima had no idea whether Mrs Parr regretted her bold leap out of the bourgeois nest. All she discovered was that Mrs Parr had had no contact whatsoever with her children for seven years. Neither sought nor proffered. Not sought because Mr Parr had confirmed Mrs Parr's suspicions by marrying Zillah the moment his divorce became absolute: 'and *she* would never have permitted it. Zillah.' Not proffered, of course, because Mrs Parr had left no address behind her.

'I had to make a new life. I wouldn't take any money from him. They'd taken my children away from me and I had to make a new life.'

It was only after the death of Mrs Parr's lover that, destitute and friendless, she had returned to England. Contacting perforce her ex-husband's lawyer for funds of some sort, she had discovered to her astonishment that Mr Parr had died suddenly several months earlier. The lawyers had been trying in their dignified and leisurely fashion to contact his first wife, the mother of his children. In the meantime the second Mrs Parr, Zillah, the children's ex-Nanny and step-mother had taken them from Sussex off to a remote corner of the Scottish Highlands. As she put it to the lawyer, she intended 'to get them and me away from it all'. The lawyer had demurred with the question of the children's future outstanding. But Zillah, with that same quiet air of authority which had swayed the divorce-court judge, convinced him. It might be months before the first Mrs Parr was contacted, she pointed out. In the meantime they had her address. And the children's.

'And suddenly there I was!' exclaimed Mrs Catharine Parr to Jemima Shore, the vehemence returning to her voice. 'But it was too late.'

'Too late?'

'Too late for Zillah. You see, Miss Shore, Zillah was dead. She was drowned in a boating accident in Scotland. It was too late for Zillah.' Jemima sensing the depth of Mrs Parr's bitterness, realized that what she really meant was: Too late for vengeance.

Even then, Mrs Parr's troubles were not over. The encounter with the children had been even more upsetting. Two children, Tamsin nearly nine and Tara nearly eight, who confronted her with scared and hostile eyes. They were being cared for at the lodge which Zillah had so precipitately rented. A local woman from the village, responsible for the caretaking of the lodge, had volunteered. Various suggestions had been made to transfer the children to somewhere less lonely, attended by less tragic memories. However, Tamsin and Tara had shown such extreme distress at the idea of moving away from their belongings and the home they knew that the plan had been abandoned. In the meantime their real mother had announced her arrival.

So Mrs Parr took the sleeper to Inverness.

'But when I got to Scotland I didn't recognize them!' cried Mrs Parr in a return to her dramatic style. 'So I want you to come back to Scotland with me and *interview* them. Find out who they are. You're an *expert* interviewer: I've seen you on television. That programme about refugee children. You talk to them. I beg you, Miss Shore. You see before you a desperate woman and a fearful mother.'

'But were you likely to recognize them?' enquired Jemima

rather dryly. 'I mean you hadn't seen either of them for seven years. How old was Tamsin then – eighteen months? Tara – what – six months?'

'It wasn't a question of *physical* recognition, I assure you. In a way, they *looked* more or less as I expected. Fair. Healthy. She'd looked after them all right, Zillah, whoever they are. She always looked after people, Zillah. That's how she got him of course.'

'Then why – ' began Jemima hastily.

Mrs Parr leant forward and said in a conspiratorial tone: 'It was spiritual recognition I meant. Nothing spoke to me and said: these are my children. In fact a voice deep in me cried out: Zillah! These are Zillah's children. This is Zillah's revenge. Even from the grave, she won't let me have my own children.' She paused for effect.

'You see Zillah had this sister Kitty. We were cousins, I think I told you. Quite close cousins even though we had been brought up so differently. That's how Zillah came to look after the children in the first place: she wanted a proper home, she said, after the impersonality of nursing. But that didn't satisfy Zillah. She was always on at me to do something about this sister and her family – as though their awful lives were my fault!'

She went on: 'Kitty had two little girls, almost exactly the same ages as my two. Quite fair then, though not as fair as Zillah and not as fair as my children. But there was a resemblance, everyone said so. People sometimes took them for my children. I suppose our relationship acounted for it. Kitty was a wretched creature but physically we were not unalike. Anyway, Zillah thought the world of these babies and was always having them round. Kitty was unhappily married: I believe the husband ran off before the last baby was born. Suddenly, looking at this pair, I thought: little cuckoos. Zillah has taken her own nieces, and put them into my nest – '

' – Which you had left of your own accord.' But Jemima did not say the words aloud. Instead she asked with much greater strength:

'But *why*?'

'The money! That's why,' exclaimed Mrs Parr in triumph. 'The Parr money in trust for them. Parr Biscuits. Doesn't that ring a bell? The money only went to the descendants of Ephraim Parr. *She* wouldn't have got a penny – except what *he* left her. Her nieces had no Parr blood either. But my children, because they were Parrs, would have been, *are* rich. Maybe my poor little children died, ran away, maybe she put them in an orphanage – *I* don't know. Or' – her voice suddenly changed totally, becoming dreamy, 'Or perhaps these are my children after all. Perhaps I'm imagining it all, after all I've been through. Miss Shore, this is just what I've come all the way from Scotland to beg you to find out.'

It was an extraordinary story. Jemima's original impulse had been to give Mrs Catharine Parr a cup of coffee and send her gently on her way. Now the overriding curiosity which was definitely her strongest attribute would not let her be. The appeals of the public to Jemima Shore Investigator certainly fell on compassionate ears; but they also fell on very inquisitive ones. In this instance she felt she owed it to the forces of common sense to point out first to Mrs Parr that lawyers could investigate such matters far more efficiently than she. To this Mrs Parr answered quite reasonably that lawyers would take an age, as they always did:

'And in the meantime what would happen to me and the children? We'd be getting to know each other, getting fond of each other. No, Miss Shore, *you* can settle it. I know you can. Then we can all get on with our lives for better or for worse.'

Then Jemima caved in and acceded to Mrs Parr's request.

It was in this way, for better or for worse as Mrs Parr had put it, that Jemima Shore Investigator found herself the following night taking the sleeper to Inverness.

The sleeping-car attendant recognized Mrs Parr quite merrily: 'Why it's you again Mrs Parr. You'll keep British Rail in business with your travelling.' Then of course he recognized Jemima Shore with even greater delight. Later, taking her ticket, he was with difficulty restrained from confiding to her his full and rich life story which he was convinced would make an excellent television documentary. Staved off, he contented himself with approving Jemima's modest order of late-night tea.

'You're not like your friend, then, Mrs Parr . . .' he made a significant drinking gesture. 'The trouble I had with her going north the first time. Crying and crying, and disturbing all the passengers. However she was better the second time, and mebbe now you'll have a good influence on her now, Miss Shore. I'll be seeing her now and asking her if this time she'll have a late-night cup of tea.' He bustled off, leaving Jemima faintly disquieted. She hoped that Mrs Parr had no drink aboard. The north of Scotland with an alcoholic, probably a fantasist into the bargain . . .

Morning found her in a more robust mood. Which was fortunate since Jemima's first sight of Kildrum Lodge, standing on the edge of a dark, seemingly endless loch, shut in by mountains, was once again disquieting. It was difficult for her to believe that Zillah could have brought the children to such a place out of sheer love for Scottish scenery and country pursuits such as fishing, swimming and walking. The situation of the lodge itself even for Scotland was so extremely isolated. Nor was the glen which led up to the lodge notably beautiful. A general lack of colour except blackness in the water reflected from the skies made it in fact peculiarly depressing. There was a lack of vegetation even on the lower slopes of the mountains, which slid down straight into the loch. The single-track road was bumpy and made of stones. It was difficult to imagine that much traffic passed that way. One could imagine a woman with something to hide – two children perhaps? – seeking out such a location, but not a warm comforting body hoping to cheer up her charges after the sudden death of their father.

The notion of Zillah's sinister purpose, far-fetched in London, suddenly seemed horribly plausible. And this was the loch, the very loch, in which Zillah herself had drowned. No, Kildrum to Jemima Shore did not have the air of a happy uncomplicated place. She looked across at Mrs Parr, in the passenger seat of the hired car. Mrs Parr looked pale. Whether she had passed the night consuming further bottles of wine or was merely dreading the next confrontation with the Parr children, the hands with which she was trying to light a cigarette were shaking. Jemima felt once more extremely sorry for her and glad that she had come to Kildrum.

They approached the lodge. It was surrounded by banks of dark-green rhododendrons, growing unrestrained, which did nothing to cheer the surroundings. There was no other garden, only rough grass going down to the loch. The large windows of the lodge looked blank and unwelcoming. As Jemima drove slowly up the stony road, the front door opened and something white was glimpsed within. It was eerily quiet once the car's engine had stopped. Then the door opened further and the flash of white proved to be a girl wearing jeans and a blue jersey. She had extremely fair, almost lint-white hair, plaited. For a girl of eight she was quite well built – even stocky.

'Tamsin,' said Mrs Parr. She pronounced the name as though for Jemima's benefit; but it was once again disquieting that she made no move towards the child. The interior of the house, like the glen itself and the mountains, was dark. Most of the paintwork was brown and the chintz curtains were patterned in a depressing brown and green. Nevertheless some energy had obviously been spent recently in making it cosy. There were cheerful traces of childish occupation, books, a bright red anorak, shiny blue gumboots. Pot plants and an arrangement of leaves bore witness to the presence of a domestic spirit in the house – once upon a time.

In the large kitchen at the back of the house where Jemima insisted on repairing for coffee there was also an unmistakable trace of modern civilization in the shape of a television set. There was a telephone too – but that was black and ancient-looking. Tamsin went with them, still silent. In the kitchen they were immediately joined by Tara, equally silent, equally blonde.

The two sisters stared warily at the women before them as if they were intruders. Which in a sense, thought Jemima, we are. Her eyes caught and held by the two striking flaxen heads, she recalled Mrs Parr's words concerning Zillah's nephew and niece: 'Quite fair too then, but not as fair as Zillah and not as fair as my children . . .' Could children actually become fairer as the years went by? Impossible. No one became fairer with time except out of a bottle. Even these children's hair was darkening slightly at the roots. Jemima felt that she had a first very positive clue that the Parr children were exactly what they purported to be. She was so relieved that a feeling of bonhomie seized her. She smiled warmly at the children and extended her hand.

'I'm Jemima Shore – '

'Investigator!' completed Tamsin triumphantly. And from her back she produced a large placard on which the cheering words: 'Welcome Jemima Shaw Investogater' were carefully inscribed in a variety of lurid pentel colours.

'I did it,' exclaimed Tara.

'I did the spelling,' said Tamsin proudly.

Jemima decided it would be tactful to congratulate her on it. At least fame on the box granted you a kind of passport to instant friendship, whatever the circumstances. In the kitchen too was another figure prepared to be an instant friend: Mrs Elspeth Maxwell, caretaker of the lodge and since the death of Zillah, *in loco parentis* to the Parr children. Elspeth Maxwell, as Jemima quickly appreciated, was a woman of uncertain age but certain garrulity. Instinctively she summed people up as to whether they would make good or bad subjects for an interview. Mrs Parr, madness and melodrama and all, would not in the end make good television. She was perhaps too obsessional at centre. But Elspeth Maxwell, under her flow of anecdote, might give you just that line or vital piece of information you needed to illuminate a whole topic. Jemima decided to cultivate her; whatever the cost in listening to a load of irrelevant gossip.

As a matter of fact Elspeth Maxwell needed about as much

cultivation as the rhododendrons growing wild outside the house. During the next few days, Jemima found that her great problem consisted in getting away from Elspeth Maxwell, who occupied the kitchen, and into the children's playroom. Mrs Parr spent most of the time in her bedroom. Her public excuse was that she wanted to let Jemima get on with her task, which had been described to Tamsin and Tara as investigation for a programme about children living in the Highlands. Privately she told Jemima that she wanted to keep clear of emotional involvement with the children 'until I'm *sure*. One way or the other.' Jemima thought there might be a third reason: that Mrs Parr wanted to consume at leisure her daily ration of cheap red wine. The pile of empty bottles on the rubbish dump beind the rhododendrons continued to grow and there was a smell of drink upstairs emanating from Mrs Parr's bedroom. Whenever Mrs Parr chose to empty an ashtray it was overflowing.

On one occasion Jemima tried the door. It was locked. After a moment Mrs Parr called out in a muffled voice: 'Go away. I'm resting.'

It was conclusive evidence of Mrs Parr's addiction that no drink was visible in the rest of the house. Jemima was never offered anything alcoholic nor was any reference made to the subject. In her experience of alcoholics, that was far more damning than the sight of a rapidly diminishing sherry bottle in the sitting-room.

Elspeth on the subject of the children was interminable: 'Ach, the poor wee things! Terrible for them, now, wasn't it? Their mother drowned before their very eyes. What a tragedy. Here in Kildrum.'

'Step-mother,' corrected Jemima. Elspeth swept on. But the tale was indeed a tragic one, whichever way you looked at it.

'A fearful accident indeed. Though there's other people been drowned in the loch, you know, it's the weeds, those weeds pull you down, right to the bottom. And it's one of the deepest lochs in the Highlands, deeper than Loch Ness, nearly as deep as Loch Morar, did you know that, Miss Shore? Then their father not so long dead, I believe, and this lady coming, their real mother, all on top of it. Then you, so famous, from television . . .'

The trouble was that for all her verbiage, Elspeth Maxwell could not really tell Jemima anything much about Zillah herself, still less about her relationship with Tamsin and Tara. It was Elspeth who had had the task of sorting out Zillah's effects and putting them into suitcases, still lying upstairs while some sort of decision was reached as to what to do with them. These Jemima made a mental note to examine as soon as possible. Otherwise Elspeth had seen absolutely nothing of Zillah during her sojourn at Kildrum Lodge.

'She wanted no help, she told the Estate Office. She could perfectly well take care of the lodge, she said, and the children. She was used to it. And the cooking. She wanted peace and quiet, she said, and to fish and walk and swim and go out in the boat – ' Elspeth stopped, 'Ah well, poor lady. But she certainly kept herself very close, herself and the children. No one knew her in Kildrum. Polite, mind you, a very polite lady, they said at the Estate Office, wrote very polite letters and notes. But very close.'

And the children? The verdict was more or less the same. Yes, they had certainly seemed very fond of Zillah whenever glimpsed in Kildrum. But generally shy, reserved. And once again polite. Elspeth could only recall one conversation of any moment before Zillah's death, out of a series of little interchanges and that was when Tamsin, in Kildrum Post Office, referred to the impending arrival of Mrs Parr. Elspeth, out of motherly sympathy for their apparent loneliness, had invited Tamsin and Tara to tea with her in the village. Tamsin had refused: 'A lady's coming from London to see us. She says she's our Mummy. But Billy and me think Zillah is our Mummy.'

It was, remarked Elspeth, an unusual burst of confidence from Tamsin. She had put it down to Tamsin's distaste at the thought of the arrival of 'the lady from London' – while of course becoming madly curious about Tamsin's family history. As a result of a 'wee discussion' of the subject in her own home, she had actually put two and two together and realized that these were the once famous Parr children. Elspeth, even in Kildrum, had naturally had strong views on *that* subject. How she would now have adored some contact with the household at Kildrum Lodge! But that was politely but steadfastly denied her. Until Zillah's death, ironically enough, brought to Elspeth exactly that involvement she had so long desired.

'I did think: mebbe she has something to hide, and my brother-in-law, Johnnie Maxwell, the ghillie, he thought mebbe the same. Keeping herself so much to herself. But all along, I dare say it was just the fear of the other mother, that one' – Elspeth rolled her eyes to the ceiling where Mrs Parr might be supposed to lie 'resting' in her bedroom – 'Fear of her finding the children. Ah well, it's difficult to judge her altogether wrong. If you know what I mean. The dreadful case. All that publicity.'

But Elspeth looked as if she would readily rehash every detail of the case of the Parr children, despite the publicity, for Jemima's benefit.

None of this was particularly helpful. Nor did inspection of Zillah's personal belongings, neatly sorted by Elspeth, bring any reward. It was not that Jemima expected to find a signed confession: 'Tamsin and Tara are imposters. They are the children of my sister . . .' Indeed, she was coming more and more to the conclusion that Mrs Parr's mad suspicions were the product of a mind disordered by alcohol. But Jemima did hope to provide herself with some kind of additional picture of the dead woman, other than the malevolent reports of the first Mrs Parr, and the second-hand gossip of Elspeth Maxwell. All she discovered was that Zillah, like Jemima herself, had an inordinate fondness for the colour beige, presumably for the same reason, to complement her fair colouring; and like a good many other English women bought her underclothes at

Marks & Spencer. Jemima did not like to speculate where and when Mrs Parr might have last bought her underclothes.

There were various photographs of Tamsin and Tara but none pre-dating Scotland. There were also some photographs of Zillah's sister Kitty; she did look vaguely like Mrs Parr, Jemima noticed, but no more than that; their features were different; it was a question of physical type rather than strict resemblance. There were no photographs of Kitty's children. Was that sinister? Conceivably. Or maybe she had merely lost touch with them. Was it also sinister that Zillah had not preserved photographs of Tamsin and Tara in Sussex? Once again: conceivably. On the other hand Zillah might have packed away all her Sussex mementoes (there were no photographs of Mr Parr either). Perhaps she came into that category of grief-stricken person who prefers not to be reminded of the past.

From the Estate Office Jemima drew another blank. Major Maclachlan, who had had the unenviable task of identifying Zillah's body, was polite enough, particularly at the thought of a television programme popularizing his corner of the Highlands. But he added very little to the public portrait of a woman whose chief characteristic was her reserve and determination to guard her privacy – her own and that of the children. Her love of country sports, especially fishing, had however impressed him: Major Maclachlan clearly found it unjust that someone with such admirable tastes should have perished as a result of them.

Only Johnnie Maxwell, Elspeth's brother-in-law who was in charge of fishing on the loch, contributed anything at all vivid to her enquiries. For it was Johnnie Maxwell who had been the principal witness at the inquest, having watched the whole drowning from the bank of the loch. To the newspaper account of the tragedy, which Jemima had read, he added some ghoulish details of the pathetic cries of the 'wee girl', unable to save Zillah. The children had believed themselves alone on the loch. In vain Johnnie had called to them to throw in the oar. Tamsin had merely screamed and screamed, oar in hand, Tara had sat quite still and silent, as though dumbstruck in horror. In their distress they did not seem to understand, or perhaps they could not hear him.

Altogether it was a most unfortunate, if not unparalleled accident. One moment Zillah was casting confidently ('Aye, she was a grand fisherwoman, the poor lady, more's the pity'). The next moment she had overbalanced and fallen in the water. There was no one else in the boat except the two children, and no one else to be seen on the shores of the loch except Johnnie. By the time he got his own boat to the children, Zillah had completely vanished and Tamsin was in hysterics, Tara quite mute. Helpers came up from the Estate. They did not find the body till the next morning, when it surfaced in the thick reeds at the shore. There were some bruises on it, but nothing that could not be explained by a fall from the boat and prolonged immersion.

That left the children. Jemima felt she owed it to Mrs Parr to cross-examine them a little on their background. Confident that she would turn up nothing to their disadvantage, she could at least reassure Mrs Parr thoroughly as a result. After that she trusted that her eccentric new contact would settle into normal life or the nearest approximation to it she could manage. Yes, the gentle, efficient cross-examination of Tamsin and Tara would be her final task and then Jemima Shore Investigator would depart for London, having closed the case of the Parr children once and for all.

But it did not work out quite like that.

The children, in their different ways, were friendly enough. Tamsin was even quite talkative once her initial shyness wore off. She had a way of tossing her head so that the blonde pigtails shook, like a show pony shaking its mane. Tara was more silent and physically frailer. But she sprang into life whenever Tamsin felt the need to contradict her, as being her elder and better. Arguing with Tamsin made even Tara quite animated. You could imagine both settling down easily once the double shock of Zillah's death and their real mother's arrival had been assimilated.

Nevertheless something was odd. It was instinct not reason that guided her. Reason told her that Mrs Parr's accusations were absurd. But then nagging instinct would not leave her in peace. She had interviewed too many subjects, she told herself, to be wrong . . . Then reason reasserted itself once more, with the aid of the children's perfectly straightforward account of their past. They referred quite naturally to their life in Sussex.

'We went to a horrid school with nasty rough boys – ' began Tara.

'It was a *lovely* school,' interrupted Tamsin, 'I played football with the boys in my break. Silly little girls like Tara couldn't do that.' All of this accorded with the facts given by the lawyer: how the girls had attended the local primary school which was fine for the tomboy Tamsin, not so good for the shrinking Tara. They would have gone to the reputedly excellent school in Kildrum when the Scottish term started had it not been for the death of Zillah.

Nevertheless something was odd, strange, not quite right.

Was it perhaps the fact that the girls never seemed to talk amongst themselves which disconcerted her? After considerable pondering on the subject, Jemima decided that the silence of Tamsin and Tara when alone – no happy or unhappy sounds coming out of their playroom or bedroom – was the most upsetting thing about them. Even the sporadic quarrelling brought on by Tamsin's bossiness ceased. Yet Jemima's experience of children was that sporadic quarrels in front of the grown-ups turned to outright war in private. But she was here as an investigator not as a child analyst (who might or might not have to follow later). Who was she to estimate the shock effect of Zillah's death, in front of their very eyes? Perhaps their confidence had been so rocked by the boating accident that they literally could not speak when alone. It was, when all was said and done, a minor matter compared to the evident correlation of the girls' stories with their proper background.

And yet . . . There was after all the whole question of

Zillah's absent nieces. Now was that satisfactorily dealt with or not? Torn between reason and instinct Jemima found it impossible to make up her mind. She naturally raised the subject, in what she hoped to be a discreet manner. For once it was Tara who answered first:

'Oh, no, we never see them. You see they went to America for Christmas and they didn't come back.' She sounded quite blithe.

'Canada, silly,' said Tamsin.

'Same thing.'

'It's not, silly.'

'It is – '

'Christmas?' pressed Jemima.

'They went for a Christmas holiday to America. Aunt Kitty took them and they never came back.'

'They went *forever*,' interrupted Tamsin fiercely. 'They went to Canada and they went *forever*. That's what Zillah said. Aunt Kitty doesn't even send us Christmas cards.' Were the answers, as corrected by Tamsin, a little too pat?

A thought struck Jemima. Later that night she consulted Mrs Parr. If Zillah's sister had been her next of kin, had not the lawyers tried to contact her on Zillah's death? Slightly reluctantly Mrs Parr admitted that the lawyers had tried and so far failed to do so. 'Oddly enough it seemed I was Zillah's next of kin after Kitty,' she added. But Kitty had emigrated to Canada (yes, Canada, Tamsin as usual was right) several years earlier and was at present address unknown. And she was supposed to have taken her two daughters with her.

It was at this point Jemima decided to throw in her hand. In her opinion the investigation was over, the Parr children had emerged with flying colours, and as for their slight oddity, well, that was really only to be expected, wasn't it? Under the circumstances. It was time to get back to Megalith Television and the autumn series. She communicated her decision to Mrs Parr, before nagging instinct could resurrect its tiresome head again.

'You don't feel it then, Jemima?' Mrs Parr sounded for the

first time neither vehement nor dreamy but dimly hopeful. 'You don't sense something about them? That they're hiding something? Something strange, unnatural . . .'

'No, I do not,' answered Jemima Shore firmly. 'And if I were you, Catharine' – they had evolved a spurious but convenient intimacy during their days in the lonely lodge – 'I would put all such thoughts behind you. See them as part of the ordeal you have suffered, a kind of long illness. Now you must convalesce and recover. And help your children, your own children, to recover too.' It was Jemima Shore at her most bracing. She hoped passionately not so much that she was correct about the children – with every minute she was more convinced of the rightness of reason, the falseness of instinct – but that Mrs Parr would now feel able to welcome them to her somewhat neurotic bosom. She might even give up drink.

Afterwards Jemima would always wonder whether these were the fatal words which turned the case of the Parr children from a mystery into a tragedy. Could she even then have realized or guessed the truth? The silence of the little girls together: did she gloss too easily over that? But by that time it was too late.

As it was, immediately Jemima had spoken, Mrs Parr seemed to justify her decision in the most warming way. She positively glowed with delight. For a moment Jemima had a glimpse of the dashing young woman who had thrown up her comfortable home to go off with the raggle-taggle-gypsies seven years before. This ardent and presumably attractive creature had been singularly lacking in the Mrs Parr she knew. She referred to herself now as 'lucky Catharine Parr', no longer the wretched Queen who lost her head. Jemima was reminded for an instant of one of the few subjects who had bested her in argument on television, a mother opposing organized schooling, like Catharine Parr a Bohemian. There was the same air of elation. The quick change was rather worrying. Lucky Catharine Parr: Jemima only hoped that she would be third time lucky as the sleeping-car attendant had suggested. It rather depended on what stability she could show as a mother.

'I promise you,' cried Mrs Parr interrupting a new train of thought, 'I give you my word. I'll never ever think about the past again. I'll look after them to my dying day. I'll give them all the love in the world, all the love they've missed all these years. Miss Shore, Jemima, I told you I trusted you. You've done all I asked you to do. Thank you, thank you.'

The next morning dawned horribly wet. It was an added reason for Jemima to be glad to be leaving Kildrum Lodge. A damp Scottish August did not commend itself to her. With nothing further to do, the dripping rhododendrons surrounding the lodge were beginning to depress her spirits. Rain sheeted down on the loch, making even a brisk walk seem impractical. With the children still silent in their playroom and Mrs Parr still lurking upstairs for the kind of late-morning rise she favoured, Jemima decided to make her farewell to Elspeth Maxwell in the kitchen.

She was quickly trapped in the flood of Elspeth's reflections, compared to which the rain outside seemed suddenly mild in contrast. Television intrigued Elspeth Maxwell in general, and Jemima, its incarnation, intrigued her in particular. She was avid for every detail of Jemima's appearance on the box, how many new clothes she needed, television make-up and so forth. On the subject of hair, she first admired the colour of Jemima's corn-coloured locks, then asked how often she had to have a shampoo, and finally enquired with a touch of acerbity:

'You'll not be putting anything on, then? I'm meaning the colour, what a beautiful bright colour your hair is, Miss Shore. You'll not be using one of those little bottles?'

Jemima smilingly denied it. 'I'm lucky.' She wasn't sure whether Elspeth believed her. After a bit Elspeth continued: 'Not like that poor lady.' She seemed obsessed with the subject. Was she thinking of dyeing her own hair? 'The late Mrs Parr, I mean, when I cleared out her things, I found plenty of bottles, different colours, dark and fair, as though she'd been making a wee experiment. And she had lovely fair hair herself, or so they said, Johnnie and the men when they took her out of the water. Just like the children. Look – ' Elspeth suddenly produced two bottles from the kitchen cupboard. One was called Goldilocks and the other Brown Leaf. Jemima thought her guess was right. Elspeth was contemplating her own wee experiment.

'I'm thinking you'll not be needing this on your *natural* fair hair.' There was a faint ironic emphasis in Elspeth's tone. 'And Tamsin and Tara, they'll have lovely hair too when they grow up. They won't need Goldilocks or such things. And who would want Brown Leaf anyway with lovely fair hair like theirs? And yours. Brown Leaf would only hide the colour.' Elspeth put the bottles back in the cupboard as though that settled the matter.

Irritated by her malice – there was nothing wrong with dyeing one's hair but Jemima just did not happen to do it – Jemima abandoned Elspeth and the kitchen for the playroom. Nevertheless, Elspeth's words continued to ring in her head. That and another remark she could not forget. Tamsin and Tara were both reading quietly, lying on their tummies on the floor. Tamsin looked up and smiled.

'When will the programme be, Miss Shore?' she asked brightly. 'When will you come back and film us? Oh, I'm so sad you're going away.'

Jemima was standing by the mantelpiece. It had a large mirror over it, which gave some light to the dark room. In the mirror she gazed back into the room, at the striking blonde heads of the two children lying on the floor. It was of course a mirror image, reversed. The sight was symbolical. It was as though for the first time she was seeing the case of the Parr children turned inside out, reversed, black white, dark fair . . . Lucky children with their mother restored to them. A mother who drank and smoked and was totally undomesticated. But was still their mother. Zillah had done none of these things – but she had done worse: she had tried to keep the children from the mother who bore them. Lucky. Third time lucky.

Jemima stood absolutely still. Behind her back Tamsin smiled again that happy innocent smile. Tara was smiling too.

'Oh yes, Miss Shore,' she echoed, 'I'm so sad you're going away'. For once Tara was in total agreement with her sister. And in the mirror Jemima saw both girls dissolve into soundless giggles, hands over their mouths to stifle the noise. She continued to stare at the children's blonde heads.

With sudden horrible clarity, Jemima knew that she was wrong, had been wrong all along. She would have to tell the woman resting upstairs that the children were not after all her own. A remark that had long haunted her came to the front of her mind. Catharine Parr: 'Just like the wretched Queen who lost her head, and I'm just as wretched.' And now she knew why it had haunted her. Catharine Parr had not been executed by Henry VIII, but she had been childless by him. Now she would have to break it to Mrs Parr that she too was childless. Would be childless in the future.

It had to be done. There was such a thing as truth. Truth – and justice. But first, however dreadfully, she had to confront the children with what they had done. She had to make them admit it.

Wheeling round, she said as calmly as possible to the little girls: 'I'm just going to drive to the telephone box to arrange with my secretary about my return. This telephone is out of order with the storm last night.' She thought she could trust Tamsin to accept the story. Then Jemima added:

'And when I come back, we'll all go out in the boat. Will you tell your – ' she paused in spite of herself, 'Will you tell your Mummy that?'

The children were not smiling now.

'The boat!' exclaimed Tamsin. 'But our Mummy can't swim. She told us.' She sounded tearful. 'She told us not to go in the boat, and anyway we don't want to. She told us we'd never ever have to go in the boat again.'

'Oh don't make us go in the horrid boat, Miss Shore,' Tara's eyes were wide with apprehension. 'Please don't. We can't swim. We never learnt yet.'

'I can swim,' replied Jemima. 'I'm a strong swimmer. Will you give your Mummy my message?'

When Jemima got back, Mrs Parr was standing with Tamsin and Tara by the door of the lodge, holding their hands (the first time Jemima had glimpsed any sign of physical affection in her). She was looking extremely distressed. She was wearing the filthy torn mackintosh in which she had first arrived at Jemima's flat. Her appearance, which had improved slightly over the last few days, was as unkempt and desperate as it had been on that weird occasion.

'Miss Shore, you mustn't do this,' she cried, the moment Jemima was out of the car. 'We can't go out in the boat. It's terrible for the children – after what happened. Besides, I can't swim – '

'I'm sorry, Catharine,' was all Jemima said. She did not relish what she had to do.

Perhaps because she was childless herself, Jemima Shaw believed passionately that young children were basically innocent whatever they did. After all, had the Parr children ever really had a chance in life since its disturbed beginnings? And now she, the alleged protector of the weak, the compassionate social campaigner, was going to administer the *coup de grâce*. She wished profoundly that she had not answered the bell to Mrs Parr that fatal Sunday morning.

The rain had stopped. The weather was clearing above the mountains in the west although the sky over the loch remained sullen. In silence the little party entered the rowing boat and Jemima pushed off from the soft ground of the foreshore.

'Come on, Tamsin, sit by me. Row like you did that afternoon with Zillah.'

Mrs Parr gave one more cry: 'Miss Shore! No.' Then she relapsed with a sort of groan into the seat at the stern of the boat. Tara sat beside her, facing Jemima and Tamsin.

After a while Jemima rested on her oar. They were near the middle of the loch. The lodge looked small and far away, the mountains behind less menacing. Following the rain the temperature had risen. Presently the sun came out. It was quite humid. Flies buzzed round Jemima's head and the children. Soon the midges would come to torture them. The water had a forbidding look: she could see thick green weeds floating just beneath the surface. An occasional fish rose and broke the black surface. No one was visible amongst the reeds. They were, the silent boat load, alone on the loch.

Or perhaps they were not alone. Perhaps Johnnie Maxwell the ghillie was somewhere amid the sedge, at his work. If so he would have seen yet another macabre sight on Loch Drum. He would have seen Jemima Shore, her red-gold hair illuminated by the sunlight, lean forward and grab Tara from her seat. He would have seen her hurl the little girl quite far into the lake, like some human Excalibur. He would have heard the loud splash, seen the spreading circles on the black water. Then he would surely, even at the edge of the loch – for the air was very still after the rain – heard Tara's cries. But even if Johnnie Maxwell had been watching, he would have been once again helpless to have saved the drowning person.

Mrs Parr gave a single loud scream and stood up at the stern of the boat. Jemima Shore sat grimly still, like a figure of vengeance. Tamsin got to her feet, wielded her oar and tried in vain to reach out to the child, splashing hopelessly now on, now under the surface of the loch. Jemima Shore continued to sit still.

Then a child's voice was heard, half choking with water: 'Zillah, save me! Zillah!'

It seemed as though the woman standing at the stern of the boat would never move. Suddenly, uncontrollably, she tore off her white mackintosh. And without further hesitation, she made a perfect racing dive on to the surface of the loch. Minutes later Tara, still sobbing and spluttering, but alive, was safely out of the water. Then for the first time since she had thrown Tara into the loch, Jemima Shore made a move – to pull the woman who had called herself Mrs Catharine Parr back into the boat again.

'The police are coming of course,' said Jemima. They were

back at the house. 'You killed her, didn't you?'

Tamsin and Tara, in dry clothes, had been sent out to play among the rhododendrons which served for a garden. The sun was gaining in intensity. The loch had moved from black to grey to slate-blue. Tara was bewildered. Tamsin was angry. 'Goodbye, *Mummy*,' she said fiercely to Zillah.

'Don't make her pretend any longer,' Jemima too appealed to Zillah. And to Tamsin: 'I know, you see. I've known for some time.'

Tamsin then turned to her sister: 'Baby. You gave it away. You promised never to call her Zillah. Now they'll come and take Zillah away. I won't ever speak to you again.' And Tamsin ran off into the dark shrubberies.

Zillah Parr, wearing some of her own clothes fished out of Elspeth's packages, was sitting with Jemima by the playroom fire. She looked neat and clean and reassuring, a child's dream mother, as she must always have looked during the last seven years. Until she deliberately assumed the messy run-down identity of Mrs Parr that is. How this paragon must have hated to dirty her finger-nails! Jemima noticed that she had seized the opportunity to scrub them vigorously while she was upstairs in the bathroom changing.

Now the mirror reflected a perfectly composed woman, legs in nice shoes, neatly crossed, sipping the glass of whiskey which Jemima had given her.

'Why not?' said Zillah coolly. 'I never drink you know, normally. Unlike *her*. Nor do I smoke. I find both things quite disgusting. As for pretending to be drunk! I used to pour all those bottles of wine down the sink. But I never found a good way of producing cigarette stubs without smoking. Ugh, the smell. I never got used to it. But I feel I may need the whiskey this afternoon.'

Silence fell between them. Then Zillah said quite conversationally: 'By the way, how did you know?'

'A historical inaccuracy was your first mistake,' replied Jemima. They might have been analysing a game of bridge. 'It always struck me as odd that a woman called Catharine Parr, an educated woman to boot, would not have known the simple facts of her namesake's life. It was Catharine Howard by the way who lost her head, not Catharine Parr.'

'Oh really.' Zillah sounded quite uninterested. 'Well I never had any education. I saw no use for it in my work, either.'

'But you made other mistakes. The sleeping-car attendant: that was a risk to take. He recognized you because of all the drinking. He spoke of you being third time lucky, and at first I thought he meant your quick journey up and down from London to Inverness and back. But then I realized that he meant that this was your third journey *northwards*. He spoke of you "going north" the second time and how you weren't so drunk as the first time. She went up first, didn't she? You killed her. Then faked your own death, and somehow got down to London secretly, perhaps from another station. Then up and down again under the name of Catharine Parr.'

'That was unlucky.' Zillah agreed. 'Of course I didn't know that he'd met the real Catharine Parr when I travelled up under her name the first time. I might have been more careful.'

'In the end it was a remark of Elspeth Maxwell's which gave me the clue. That, and your expression.'

'That woman! She talks far too much,' said Zillah with a frown.

'The dyes: she showed me the various dyes you had used, I suppose to dye Mrs Parr's hair blonde and darken your own.'

'She dyed her own hair,' Zillah sounded positively complacent. 'I've always been good at getting people to do things. I baited her. Pointed out how well I'd taken care of myself, my hair still blonde and thick, and what a mess she looked. Why, I looked more like the children's mother than she did. I knew that would get her. We'd once been awfully alike, you see, at least to look at. You never guessed that, did you? Kitty never really looked much like her, different nose, different shaped face. But as girls, Catharine and I were often mistaken for each other. It even happened once or twice when I was working for her. And how patronizing she was about it. "Oh no, that was just Zillah" she used to say with that awful laugh of hers when she'd been drinking "Local saint and poor relation". I was like her but not like.' Zillah hesitated and then went on more briskly.

'I showed her the bottle of Goldilocks, pretended I used it myself and she grabbed it. "Now we'll see who the children's real mother is" she said, when she'd finished.'

'The bottle did fool me at first,' admitted Jemima. 'I thought it must be connected somehow with the children's hair. Then Elspeth gave me the key when she wondered aloud who would ever use Brown Leaf if they had fair hair: "It would only hide the colour." She paused. 'So you killed her, blonde hair and all.'

'Yes I killed her,' Zillah was still absolutely composed. She seemed to have no shame or even fear. 'I drowned her. She was going to take the children away. I found out that she couldn't swim, took her out in the boat in the morning when I knew Johnnie Maxwell wasn't around. Then I let her drown. I would have done anything to keep the children,' she added.

'I told the children that she'd gone away,' she went on. 'That horrid drunken old tramp. Naturally I didn't tell them I'd killed her. I just said that we would play a game. A game in which I would pretend to fall into the lake and be drowned. Then I would dress up in her old clothes and pretend to *be* her. And they must treat me just as if I *was* her, all cold and distant. They must never hug me as if I was Zillah. And if they played it properly, if they never talked about it to anyone, not even to each other when they were alone, the horrid mother would never come back. And then I could be their proper mother. Just as they had always wanted. Zillah, they used to say with their arms round me, we love you so much, won't you be our Mummy for ever?' Her voice became dreamy and for a moment Zillah was reminded of the person she had known as Catharine Parr. 'I couldn't have any children of my own, you see; I had to have an operation when I was quite young. Wasn't it unfair? That she could have them, who was such a terrible mother, and I couldn't. All my life I've always loved other people's children. My sister's. Then his children.'

'It was the children all along, wasn't it? Not the money. The Parr Trust: that was a red herring.'

'The money!' exclaimed Zillah. Her voice was full of contempt. 'The Parr Trust meant nothing to me. It was an encumbrance if anything. Little children don't need money: they need love and that's exactly what I gave to them. And she would have taken them away, the selfish good-for-nothing tramp that she was, that's what she threatened to do, take them away, and never let me see them again. She said in her drunken way, laughing and drinking together. "This time my fine cousin Zillah, the law will be on my side." So I killed her. And so I defeated her. Just as I defeated her the last time when she tried to take the children away from me in court.'

'And from their father,' interposed Jemima.

'The judge knew a real motherly woman when he saw one,' Zillah went on as though she had not heard. 'He said so in court for all the world to hear. And he was right, wasn't he? Seven years she left them. Not a card. Not a present. And then thinking she could come back, just like that, because their father was dead, and claim them. All for an accident of birth. She was nothing to them, *nothing*, and I was everything.'

And Jemima herself? Her mission?

'Oh yes, I got you here deliberately. To test the children. I was quite confident, you see. I knew they would fool you. But I wanted them to know the sort of questions they would be asked – by lawyers, even perhaps the Press. I used to watch you on television,' she added with a trace of contempt. 'I fooled that judge. He never knew about their father and me. I enjoy fooling people when it's necessary. I knew I could fool you.'

'But you didn't,' said Jemima Shore coldly. She did not like the idea of being fooled. 'There was one more clue. An expression. The expression of triumph on your face when I told you I was satisfied about the children and was going back to London. You dropped your guard for a moment. It reminded me of a woman who had once scored over me on television. I didn't forget that.' She added, 'Besides, you would never have got away with it.'

But privately she thought that if Zillah Parr had not displayed her arrogance by sending for Jemima Shore Investigator as a guinea pig she might well have done so. After all no one had seen Catharine Parr for seven years; bitterly she had cut herself off completely from all her old friends when she went to Ireland. Zillah had also led a deliberately isolated life after her husband's death; in her case she had hoped to elude the children's mother should she ever reappear. Zillah's sister had vanished to Canada. Elspeth Maxwell had been held at arm's length as had the inhabitants of Kildrum. Johnnie Maxwell had met Zillah once but there was no need for him to meet the false Mrs Parr, who so much disliked fishing.

The two women were much of an age and their physical resemblance in youth striking: that resemblance which Zillah suggested had first attracted Mr Parr towards her. Only the hair had to be remedied, since Catharine's untended hair had darkened so much with the passing of the years. As for the corpse, the Parr family lawyer, whom Zillah had met face to face at the time of her husband's death, was, she knew, on holiday in Greece. It was not difficult to fake a resemblance sufficient to make Major Maclachlan at the Estate Office identify the body as that of Zillah Parr. The truth was so very bizarre: he was hardly likely to suspect it. He would be expecting to see the corpse of Zillah Parr, following Johnnie's account, and the corpse of Zillah Parr, bedraggled by the loch, he would duly see.

The unkempt air of a tramp was remarkably easy to assume: it was largely a matter of externals. After a while the new Mrs Catharine Parr would have discreetly improved her appearance. She would have left Kildrum – and who would have blamed her? – and started a new life elsewhere. A new life with the children. Her own children: at last.

As all this was passing through Jemima's head, suddenly Zillah's control snapped. She started to cry: 'My children, my children. Not hers, Mine – ' And she was still crying when the police car came up the rough drive, and tall men with black and white check bands round their hats took her away. First they had read her the warrant: 'Mrs Zillah Parr, I charge you with the murder of Mrs Catharine Parr, on or about the morning of August 6 . . . at Kildrum Lodge, Inverness-shire.'

As the police car vanished from sight down the lonely valley, Tara came out of the rhododendrons and put her hand in Jemima's. There was no sign of Tamsin.

'She will come back, Miss Shore, won't she?' she said anxiously. 'Zillah, I mean, not that Mummy. I didn't like that Mummy. She drank bottles all the time and shouted at us. She said rude words, words we're not allowed to say. I cried when she came and Tamsin hid. That Mummy even tried to hit me. But Zillah told us she would make the horrid Mummy go away. And she did. When will Zillah come back, Miss Shore?'

Holding Tara's hand, Jemima reflected sadly that the case of the Parr children was probably only just beginning.

Swimming Will Be The Death Of You

'All I say,' declared Mrs Bancroft to Jemima Shore Investigator, 'is that swimming can damage your health. Just like cigarettes. I mean, look at the way you do it, winter and summer. No regard to the seasons. Rain or shine. Hot or cold. Unnatural I call it.'

'It's indoors, Mrs B.,' replied Jemima Shore patiently. 'You know, Holland Pools across the road. It's Keep Fit, that's the point. Unwinding after doing the programme. It's far the best quick way of taking exercise. Plenty of people do it these days all the year round.'

Jemima Shore sounded patient because she was in fact feeling rather impatient with Mrs B., her beloved but highly possessive cleaning lady. Life working for Megalith Television as an investigative reporter would be quite impossible without Mrs B., as Jemima was well aware; on the other hand she was longing to get on with the revised script for her new programme on the problems of the working housewife, tentative title: 'House Unbound'.

'Plenty of people are not Jemima Shore Investigator!' exclaimed Mrs B. indignantly. 'Look at that cough you went and got when you were interviewing that poor Asian woman! Everyone was talking about it the next day. Now that was swimming, I bet. No one should swim with a hacking cough – '

'Mrs B.,' cried Jemima, putting down the script, 'you've just reminded me. I promised Mrs Robertson I'd meet her at Holland Pools for a spot of Keep Fit – ' She jumped up, hoping Mrs B. would not detect the white lie.

'Jemima Shore,' pronounced Mrs B. darkly as she watched Jemima hastily grabbing a bright pink towel and black costume, 'swimming will be the death of you.'

Not much later Jemima was reminded of Mrs B.'s dedicated opposition to swimming as a pastime as she changed in one of the narrow cubicles of Holland Pools. Someone near her definitely had a hacking cough of the kind that would have appalled Mrs B. Jemima could not however see who the unfortunate cougher was; it had to be a woman, or rather a female, since a stern notice over the door of this, the right-hand changing-room on the way to the pools, commanded: 'No boys except infants'. ('Mum, aren't I a boy?' she heard a little boy ask anxiously as she was swept through the swing doors.)

Jemima could not catch a glimpse of the cougher because the cubicles were so constructed that the shiny white walls went all the way about the changers' heads, leaving, however, a wide gap at the bottom showing the feet. Jemima stooped to pick up her cotton-knit jersey from the floor: to her annoyance it had fallen in a puddle, for the cubicles were often very wet by this time of day. It was then that she noticed to her surprise that there were two pairs of feet instead of one to be seen on the floor of the next-door cubicle.

How odd! Then: schoolgirls larking about, she thought. A number of neighbourhood schools took their pupils to swim at Holland Pools. Jemima was used to the bustle of raucous-voiced swimming teachers, male and female, shouting at recalcitrant figures shivering on the brink. When she arrived in the changing-room a group of black girls had been playing an elaborate game of tag in and out of the cubicles. Jemima judged them to be ten or eleven, and thought how pretty they looked, even in the plain school bathing-costume, with their slim athletic figures and long legs. Mrs Ruby, however, the massive figure in jeans and scarlet T-shirt emblazoned HOLLAND POOLS HELPER who was this afternoon in charge of the changing-room, took a sterner view.

'No running! No shouting!' Mrs Ruby called out from time to time, in a voice which was itself close to a shout. Mrs Ruby and Jemima had become good friends. Mrs Ruby was essentially motherly and in some ways reminded Jemima of Mrs B. Jemima knew all about Mrs Ruby's son Michael who still lived with her despite his marriage, and Mrs Ruby's daughter Dilys who also lived at home without however being married. Indeed Jemima knew Dilys personally since Dilys, built on the same cheerful scale as her mother but with a mercifully softer voice, also worked at the pools. The two women, along with the others, worked in a rota which meant that they sometimes oversaw the changing-rooms, and with the aid of lifeguards, sometimes the pools themselves. Looking at Mrs Ruby and Dilys, Jemima could well believe that both were excellent swimmers, competent to save any life in any crisis.

Jemima also knew Mrs Ruby's unsatisfactory daughter-in-law, Lisa, she who refused to provide Mrs Ruby with grandchildren.

'Though as they're living with me in my nice house,' pointed out Mrs Ruby, 'I could look after the kids, with me a widow, built-in baby-sitter, that's what they've got. They'll get the house when I'm gone of course, but I've a good few years in me yet. The trouble is, Lisa has it too soft. Michael worships her. Gives *her* all his money; no rent for me, always says he will, then he's short. Dilys and I are quite fed up with her, I can tell you.'

Jemima could not help noticing how Lisa, the outsider, took all the blame for Michael's financial failure. Yet surely it was as much, if not more, Michael's fault as Lisa's that he paid no rent? As for Lisa, Jemima could hardly blame her if she did not consider a house shared with a disapproving mother-in-law as the ideal nest in which to raise children. The truth was that Mrs Ruby, and Dilys as well, had never really forgiven Michael, their spoilt darling, for marrying in the first place; Jemima secretly pitied poor Lisa for being at the mercy of two such formidable women.

'Sometimes I really *hate* her,' Mrs Ruby burst out with surprising vehemence for one normally so kind. 'When I think how happy we all were. Me and Dilys and Michael. We just fitted in so snugly together at home. And then *she* came. This morning, for example, I could have cheerfully strangled her – Michael has to bring her breakfast in bed – *and* get off to work – '

No, Jemima did not envy the fate of Mrs Ruby's daughter-in-law. Yet Lisa herself was, to Jemima at least, a rather beguiling creature, even if her interests did not seem to extend much beyond the music she listened to on her Sony Walkman, while cultivating a tan in the Sun Lounge next to the big pool. Jemima often noticed her there, blonde streaked hair piled high, leopard-skin bikini or something similarly exotic, leaving little of the tan to the imagination. Accompanied by a girl called Gretel, who might have been her sister so far as hair-style and bikini-style were concerned, Lisa could be seen chatting to, and being chatted up by, various hunks of male beefcake, whose wondrously bronze torsos and constant presence at all hours of the day suggested that they were unemployed and making the best of it. Gretel was shyer; Lisa gazed at the young men, but Gretel gazed at Lisa.

'No running!' bellowed Mrs Ruby for the third time. 'Can't you kids read the notice?' Looking at the notice herself, Jemima was suddenly aware how many of the notices pinned up around her were warnings. Most of them seemed to begin: 'Beware'. For example: 'Beware pickpockets', 'Beware leaving valuables in your locker', 'Beware taking a hot shower' – now what was wrong with that? – ah – 'Turn on the cold tap first'. And these were just in the changing-room. On the way to the pools were a series of other notices equally peremptory. 'No entry under any circumstances' – a staff-room – was simple enough. Beside the pool itself, 'Steep slope' and 'Deep water' were perhaps only mildly menacing. But 'Warning to swimmers' and 'What to do if you get into trouble swimming' sounded a genuinely threatening note. Most threatening of all – and the largest notice, with red lettering to emphasize it – read: 'A loud siren means GET OUT OF THE WATER. That means you. Get out at once.'

Jemima pondered on this as she changed into her costume: silky black, cut away very high indeed at the sides to make her legs look, she hoped, as long as a dancer's. Wryly she wondered whether swimming was really the innocent Keep Fit exercise she had always supposed. How many things could go wrong! Into these thoughts a low voice from the next-door cubicle cut in so appropriately that for a moment she almost believed she had imagined it.

'Too dangerous,' said the voice, so low that it was not much more than a whisper. 'Not here, I'd never dare. Not here.'

'You can,' came the answer. 'You *can*.'

Afterwards Jemima worked out that the noise of the schoolchildren in and out of the cubicles had masked the sound of her own arrival. In any case she had chosen a group of cubicles slightly isolated from the main block to get away from the girls' games (and Mrs Ruby's voice). The heavy steel lockers in which everyone was supposed to store clothes while swimming, hid these cubicles from the central desk and showers.

Now Jemima remained frozen. Was she to emerge from her cubicle and store her clothes in the locker opposite? (Its number was on the white rubber band round her wrist.) In which case she would not be able to see the face or faces of the persons in the next-door cubicle, unless all parties emerged together, which was unlikely. Curiosity, her besetting sin (or virtue, depending on your point of view) made her hesitate . . . who was it who had whispered such a very surprising and once again ominous remark – and to whom?

It was suddenly very quiet in the changing-room as a whole. The girls had roistered off in the direction of the pool, the noise of their cries and giggles gradually swallowed up in the general pool noises. Even Mrs Ruby was silent. While Jemima hesitated, she heard the sound of the adjacent door opening, and before she had time to amass her own bundle of clothes, there was the soft patter of feet. No lockers slammed. Whoever her mysterious neighbours were, they were not using lockers 200 to 250. Other than the fact that according to their feet, they were female, Jemima knew nothing else about them; she did not know what it was that was so dangerous to accomplish.

Jemima decided to put the whole incident out of her mind. After all, swimming was not only about keeping physically fit, it was also about mental peace and relaxation. Doing her laps in a graceful not too energetic crawl up and down the pool, Jemima concentrated on relaxing – even if that was a slight contradiction in terms. At the shallow end, the school-girls were continuing their larks; occasionally one of the bigger ones swam up to the deep end and performed a perfect swallow dive. Another class of children, boys as well as girls, were learning life-saving. Every now and then a pair, wearing incongruous cotton pyjamas or flowered dresses, would jump in with a great splash and one would 'rescue' the other.

The adult swimmers were much less in evidence. Many of them wore goggles against the chlorine, which made it even impossible to be certain about their sex once they were in the water. Jemima herself hated chlorine but hated bathing caps and goggles more; she generally pinned her golden-red hair up and washed it out under the shower later. It was when one swimmer suddenly said: 'Hello, Jemima', that she wished that the flamboyant colour of her hair was not quite so recognizable. Then to her surprise Jemima found herself alongside Lisa Ruby, swimming a fast but jerky breast stroke. What was more, Gretel was there too, swimming gamely alongside like a sister ship.

Lisa made a grimace.

'I don't know about you, Jemima,' she panted, 'but I don't think this is any fun. Keep Fit! Keep Cold, more likely. Still' –

she indicated Mrs Ruby, whose scarlet T-shirt could now be seen on the edge of the pool – '*Mum* said I had to do it. Said I couldn't just lie about in the Sun Lounge. I must swim today. What business is it of hers? Oh well, anything for peace . . .' It was true that Lisa was puffing quite heavily. Gretel swam more easily. But then she was not trying to talk at the same time.

Jemima, who was heading in the opposite direction, crawled on, while Lisa, accompanied by the faithful Gretel, continued to chug forward to where the children were learning life-saving. Jemima decided to put the encounter with Lisa out of her mind as well. Keep Fit, relax, relax . . . She did a couple of lengths without noticing anything very much except the ripple of the light azure water ahead as her arm cleaved through it.

It was because her head was more than half buried in the water that at first she did not appreciate the sound of the siren for what it was. Suddenly the ugly blaring urgent message reached her. Feeling guilty because she must have swum on when a swimmer was somewhere in trouble, Jemima speeded up her pace and raced to the steps at the shallow end. Clambering out, she grabbed her shocking-pink towel with its striking js logo and draped herself hastily in it. She found herself amid a crowd of dripping children being assembled into some kind of order by the raucous-voiced teacher. Then she looked round. The pool was now all but empty as the last adult swimmers removed themselves. But the boys and girls in the life-saving class were all still up at the deep end, many of them dripping wet in their baggy cotton clothes. It was, however, somewhere up that end that the commotion or incident or whatever it was had evidently taken place.

The siren, mercifully, stopped at last. Then in the new silence could be heard the sound of a woman's voice screaming over and over again: 'She tried to kill me, she did, she tried to kill me, she did . . .' After a while the voice itself was interrupted by a horrendous fit of coughing and spluttering.

Jemima could now see quite clearly the figure of Lisa Ruby,

recognizable more by her leopard-skin bikini than by her streaky blonde top-knot, since her hair was now streaming down her back in a bedraggled mass. A man, presumably a lifeguard, wearing a HOLLAND POOLS T-shirt and black trunks, put a red towel round Lisa and started to lead her away. Gretel, already draped in a red towel, trailed after her.

Ignoring Lisa's hysterical words – for hysterical they surely were – Jemima felt relief that the siren just meant some kind of little incident in the pool, from which Lisa had clearly emerged with nothing worse than a ruined hair-style. It was time to go and change. In spite of Mrs B.'s gloomy prediction, swimming had not been the death of her (nor anyone else, fortunately) but it might be the making of a very nasty cold if she hung about much longer in a wet costume.

It was only now that the continued presence of a knot of people, including some of the children, at the head of the pool, struck her as unnatural and disquieting. Then the children moved away and the centre of the knot was revealed to her. Jemima saw with a sick feeling that there was something lying flat and unmoving on the side of the pool with a person kneeling over it, kneading it, pumping it, rhythmically hitting it. The person kneading and hitting was wearing a red T-shirt; from the heavy figure and short hair Jemima knew it was Dilys Ruby. The inanimate object was also wearing a red shirt and was also very heavy. With mounting horror Jemima realized the object was Mrs Ruby herself.

Some time later, when Mrs Ruby's sodden and lifeless body had been taken away in an ambulance, accompanied by a distraught Dilys, it was still rather difficult to make out exactly what had happened. A chapter of accidents, or rather unfortunate coincidences, was the general shocked verdict on Mrs Ruby's death: although there would of course be a full enquiry into the exact circumstances which had led up to it.

It all began when Lisa Ruby got into difficulties, on that at least everyone was agreed. Had Lisa's difficulties been brought on by two children from the life-saving class jumping in far too close to her as Gretel suggested? Or had Lisa herself accidentally swum too close to the class area as the teacher indignantly countered? At all events Lisa became as she put it, 'absolutely swamped: my mouth filled with water: I was drowning.'

'So what was a poor swimmer like her doing up the deep end in the first place?' demanded the teacher angrily. To which Lisa, weeping and coughing at the same time, responded: '*She* made me, it was all her idea, Mum's idea.'

At this point the presence of the children splashing about and practising life-saving proved to be the most unfortunate coincidence. Normally the lifeguards would have been instantly alert to any splashing and Lisa would have been rapidly rescued, towed to the side. As it was, Lisa's struggles passed unnoticed for a few critical moments.

It was Mrs Ruby, who had just taken leave of Dilys, on her way to the staff-room for a cup of tea, who saw what was going on and jumped in. Even then all might have been well, since Mrs Ruby was a proficient swimmer and life-saver. But somehow the splashing children, the choking Lisa, Gretel ineffectively trying to save her friend although a very poor swimmer herself, and Mrs Ruby all became fatally entangled. Those children who ambitiously sought to use their new-found skill of rescue only added to the confusion.

Then it was, according to Lisa, that Mrs Ruby turned from would-be saviour into would-be slayer. Only the lethal struggle had somehow gone wrong and by the time the lifeguard reached them, with the siren urgently sounding, it was Lisa who was able to be rescued and Mrs Ruby who was not.

Jemima gazed in pity at Lisa's pathetic little tear-blotched face, damp blonde hair screwed back again into a tight little knot. She thought of the terrifying destructive power of family hatreds; how Mrs Ruby's jealousy and resentment of her daughter-in-law must have suddenly crystallized into an overwhelming impulse to remove her for ever from her life – and Michael's life, and Mrs Ruby's house. 'Yesterday morning I could cheerfully have strangled her' – that was Mrs

Ruby to Jemima. Unbidden, those other sinister words overheard by Jemima in the cubicle floated in her mind: 'Too dangerous . . . not here' and then: 'You can. You *can*.' If one voice was Mrs Ruby, her warm and motherly Mrs Ruby, then the other must by implication have been her daughter Dilys.

These thoughts were interrupted by a fresh bout of coughing from Lisa. Gretel, sitting beside her (both girls were still wrapped in the red Holland Pools towels) put her arm round Lisa's shoulder in comfort. Jemima looked down. The girls were too shocked even to put on shoes, let alone to dress. At which point Jemima found her thoughts being diverted in a strange new direction by the familiar affectionate nagging voice of Mrs B. 'No-one should swim with a hacking cough.' And the memory of a white-tiled floor.

I'm going to follow it through, she promised herself: there's something wrong here. Mrs Ruby, that bossy woman, why did she choose today to make Lisa go for a swim? When Lisa's ill-health, cosseted by Michael, was already causing her annoyance. Then Jemima looked down at the floor again. Swimming in that state could be the death of you; but it wasn't the death of Lisa, was it? it was the death of Mrs Ruby . . .

She began to think all over again of the cubicle conspiracy: 'Not here. Too dangerous.' And another voice urging her on. 'You can. *You can*.' She thought of the terrible power of an apparently weak swimmer calling for help; choosing her exact moment when Mrs Ruby was passing close on the brink, and her exact place in the midst of the confusion of the life-saving class. A weak swimmer with a heavy cough which gave plausibility to her dramatic gulping.

'Swimming will be the death of you.' Looking down at the floor, Jemima knew that she was looking at the two pairs of feet which had inhabited the next door cubicle. It was Lisa and Gretel who had made sure that Lisa's swimming would be the death of Mrs Ruby.

'The house,' said Jemima slowly. 'You couldn't wait, could you? The house and Michael. She grumbled about you, but you hated her. And so you trapped her between you. And you drowned her.'

'It's not true, it's not true!' Lisa shrieked, and she started to cry again. Fatally she added before Gretel could stop her: 'You can't prove it, you can't prove anything.'

'Maybe not at the moment, here in the changing-room,' said Jemima Shore grimly, 'but once we've all got our clothes on, I'm going to have a very good try.'

Your Appointment is Cancelled

'This is Arcangelo's Salon, Epiphany speaking. I am very sorry to inform you that your appointment is cancelled . . .' In sheer surprise, Jemima Shore looked at the receiver in her hand. But still the charming voice went on. After a brief click, the message started all over again. 'This is Arcangelo's Salon, Epiphany speaking. I am very sorry to inform you that your appointment is cancelled . . .'

In spite of the recording, Jemima imagined Epiphany herself at the other end of the telephone – the elegant black receptionist with her long neck and high cheekbones. Was she perhaps Ethiopian, Somali, or from somewhere else in Africa, which produced such beauties? Wherever she came from, Epiphany looked, and probably was, a princess. She was also, on the evidence of her voice and manner, highly educated; there was some rumour at the salon that Epiphany had been to university.

As the message continued on its level way, Jemima thought urgently: What about my hair? She touched the thick reddish-gold mass whose colour and various styles had been made famous by television. Jemima thought it was professional to take as much trouble about her hair as she did about the rest of the details concerning her celebrated programme looking into the social issues of the day, Jemima Shore Investigates. She had just returned from filming in Morocco (working title: New Women of the Kasbah) and her hair was in great need of the attentions of Mr Leo, the Italian proprietor of Arcangelo's – or, failing that, those of his handsome English son-in-law, Mr Clark.

But her appointment was cancelled and Jemima wondered what had happened at Arcangelo's.

A few hours later, the *London Evening Post* ran a brief front-page bulletin: a male hair-stylist at a certain fashionable salon had been found when the salon opened that morning with his head battered in by some form of blunt instrument. The police, led by Jemima's old friend, Detective Chief Inspector J. H. Portsmouth – more familiarly known as Pompey of the Yard – were investigating.

As Jemima was mulling this over, she received a phone call from Mr Leo who told her in a flood of Italianate English that the dead stylist was none other than his son-in-law, and that it was he, Leo, who had discovered the body when he unlocked the salon this morning. Epiphany, who normally did the unlocking, having been delayed on the Underground.

'Miss Shore,' he ended brokenly, 'they are thinking it is I, Leo, who am doing this dreadful thing, I who am killing Clark. Because of her, *mia cara, mia figlia, Domenica mia*. And yes, it is true, he was not a good husband, in spite of all I did for him, all she has been doing for him. In spite of the *bambino!*'

He paused and went on as though reluctantly. 'A good stylist yes, it is I who have taught him. Yes, he is good. Not as good as me, no, who would say that? But good. But he was a terrible husband. *Un marito abominabile.* I knew, of course. How could I not know? Everyone, even the juniors knew, working in the salon all day together. *My* salon! The salon *I* have created, I, Leo Vecchetti. They thought they were so clever. Clever! Bah!

'But for that I would not have killed him. She still loved him, my daughter, my only child. For her I built up everything, I did it all. My child, Domenica, and the little one,

Leonella, who will come after her. Now he is dead and the police think I did it. Because I'm Italian and he's English. You Sicilians, they say. But I'm not Sicilian. I'm from the North, *sono Veneziano* – ' Mr Leo gave an angry cry and the flood poured on:

'What about *her* then?' he almost shouted. 'Maybe *she* killed him because he would not leave Domenica and marry her!' He now sounded bitter as well as enraged. 'No, Clark would not leave my fine business – the business he would one day inherit. Not for one of those *savages*, not he. Maybe *she* kill him – kill him with a *spear* like in the *films!*'

From this, Jemima wondered if Leo was saying that Epiphany had been Mr Clark's mistress.

'Mr Leo,' she said. 'When the salon reopens, I want an immediate appointment.'

A few days later, Jemima drew up at Arcangelo's in her white Mercedes sports car. The golden figure of an angel blowing a trumpet over the entrance made the salon impossible to miss. Jemima was put in a benign mood by being able to grab a meter directly outside the salon from under the nose of a rather flashy-looking Jaguar being propelled at a rather more dignified pace by its male driver. She glimpsed purple-faced anger, rewarded it with a ravishing smile, and was rewarded in turn by the driver's startled recognition of the famous television face.

Well, I've certainly lost a fan there, thought Jemima cheerfully. She looked through the huge plate-glass window and saw Epiphany, on the telephone, austerely beautiful in a high-necked black jersey. One of the other stylists – Mr Roderick, she thought his name was – was bending over her. Epiphany was indeed alluring enough to make a man lose his head.

Pompey of the Yard, being a good friend of Jemima's from several previous co-operations beneficial to both sides, had filled in a few more details of the murder for Jemima. The blunt instrument had turned out to be a heavy metal hair-dryer. Mr Clark's body had been found – a macabre touch –

sitting under one of the grey-and-gold automatic dryers. The medical examiner estimated the time of death as between ten and eleven the previous evening, more likely later than earlier because of the body temperature. The salon closed officially at about six, but the staff sometimes lingered until six-thirty or thereabouts, tending to each other's hair – cutting, restyling, putting in highlights, unofficial activities they had no time for during the day.

The night of the murder, Mr Clark had offered to lock up the salon. (Being one of the senior stylists and, of course, Mr Leo's son-in-law, he possessed his own set of keys.) At five o'clock, he had telephoned Domenica at home and told her he had a last-minute appointment: he had to streak the hair of a very important client and he might be home very late because this client was then going to take him to some film gala in aid of charity, to which she needed an escort – he couldn't offend her by refusing. Domenica, brought up in the hairdressing business and used to such last-minute arrangements, had a late supper with Clark's sister Janice, who had come to admire the baby, and went to bed alone. When she woke up in the morning and found Mr Clark still absent, she simply assumed, said Pompey of the Yard with a discreet cough, that the party had gone on until morning.

'Some client!' said Jemima indignantly. 'I suppose you've questioned her. The client, I mean.'

'I'm doing so now,' Pompey had told her, with another discreet cough. 'You see, the name of the famous client whose offer Mr Clark simply could not refuse, according to his wife, was *yours*. It was you who was supposed to have come in at the last minute, needing streaks in a hurry before beginning the new series.'

'Needing streaks *and* an escort, to say nothing of what else I was supposed to need,' commented Jemima grimly. 'Well, of all the cheek – '

'*We* think,' Pompey had interposed gently into Jemima's wrath, 'he had a date with the black girl there at the salon after everybody had gone. There is a beautician's room which is quite spacious and comfortable, couch and all. And very private after hours.'

'All very nice and convenient,' Jemima said, still smarting from the late Mr Clark's impudence. 'So that's where they were in the habit of meeting.'

'We think so. And we think Mr Leo knew that – and, being Sicilian and full of vengeance – '

'He's Venetian actually.'

'Being *Venetian* and full of vengeance. There's plenty of vengeance in Venice, Jemima. Have you ever been to the place? Mrs Portsmouth and I went once and when you encounter those gondoliers – ' He broke off and resumed a more official tone. 'Whatever his genesis, we believe he decided to tackle his son-in-law. That is to say, we think he killed him with several blows with a hair-dryer.

'Mr Leo has no alibi after nine o'clock. After a quick supper at home, he went out – he says –to the local pub, returning after it closed. But nobody saw him in the pub and he is, as you know, a striking-looking man. He had plenty of time to get to the salon, kill his son-in-law, and get back home.'

'What about Epiphany? Mr Leo blames her.'

'She admits to having been the deceased's mistress – she could hardly deny it when everybody at the salon knew. She even admits to having an occasional liaison with him at the salon in the evening. But on this particular evening, she says very firmly that she went to the cinema – alone. She's given us the name of the film. *Gandhi*. All very pat. What's more, the commissionaire remembers her in the queue – she is, after all, a very beautiful woman –and so does the girl at the box office. The only thing is, she had plenty of time once the film was over to get back to the salon and kill her lover.'

'She has no alibi for her activities after the movie?' put in Jemima.

'Not really. She lives with a girl friend off the Edgware Road. But the friend's away – a very convenient fact if there was anything sinister going on – so according to Epiphany she just went home after the cinema, had a bit of supper, got into her lonely bed, and slept. Saw no one. Talked to no one. Telephoned no one. As for being late the next morning, that, too, was a piece of luck – stoppage on the Underground. We've checked that, of course, and it's true enough. But she could have come by a slower route, or even just left home later than usual so as to avoid opening up the shop and seeing the grisly consequences of her deed. As it was, we were there before she arrived.'

With this information in her head, Jemima now entered the salon. Epiphany gave her usual calm welcome, asking the nearest junior – Jason, who had a remarkable coxcomb of multi-coloured hair – to take Miss Shore's coat and lead her to the basin. But Jemima didn't think it was her imagination that made her suppose Epiphany was frightened under her placid exterior. Of course, she could well be mourning her lover (presuming she had not killed him, and possibly even if she had) but Jemima's instinct told her there was something beyond that – something that was agitating, even terrifying Epiphany.

In the cloakroom, Pearl, another junior with a multi-coloured mop, took Jemima's fleecy white fur.

'Ooh, Miss Shore, how do you keep it so clean? It's white fox, is it?'

'I dump it in the bath,' replied Jemima with perfect truth. 'Not white fox – white nylon.'

At the basin, Jason washed her hair with his usual scatty energy and later Mr Leo set it. Mr Leo was not scatty in any sense of the word. He did the set, as ever, perfectly, handling the thick rollers handed to him by Jason so fast and yet so deftly that Jemima, with much experience in having her hair done all over the world, doubted whether anyone could beat Mr Leo for speed or expertise.

Nevertheless, she sensed beneath his politeness, as in Epiphany, all the tension of the situation. The natural self-discipline of the professional hairdresser able to make gentle, interested conversation with the client whatever his own personal problems: in this case, a son-in-law brutally

77

murdered, a daughter and grandchild bereft, himself the chief suspect, to say nothing of the need to keep the salon going smoothly if the whole family business was not to collapse.

At which point Mr Leo suddenly confounded all Jemima's theories about this unassailable professionalism by thrusting a roller abruptly back into Jason's hand.

'You finish this,' he commanded. And with a very brief, muttered excuse in Jemima's general direction, he darted off toward the reception desk. In the mirror before her, Jemima was transfixed to see Mr Leo grab a dark-haired young woman by the shoulder and shake her while Epiphany, like a carved goddess, stared enigmatically down at the appointments book on her desk as though the visitor and Mr Leo did not exist. But it was interesting to note that the ringing telephone, which she normally answered at once, clamoured for at least half a minute before it claimed her attention.

The young woman and Mr Leo were speaking intensely in rapid Italian. Jemima spoke some Italian but this was far too quick and idiomatic for her to understand even the gist of it.

Then Jemima recognized the distraught woman – Domenica, Mr Leo's daughter. And at the same moment she remembered that Domenica had worked as receptionist at the salon before Epiphany. Had she met Mr Clark there? Probably. And probably left the salon to look after the baby, Leonella. It was ironic that it was Epiphany who had turned up to fill the gap. But why had Domenica come to the salon today? To attack Epiphany? Was that why Mr Leo was hustling her away to the back of the salon with something that looked very much like force?

Jason had put in the last roller and fastened some small clips on the tendrils Jemima sometimes liked to wear at her neck. Now he fastened the special silky Arcangelo's net like a golden filigree over her red hair and led Jemima to the dryers with his usual energetic enthusiasm. Jason was a great chatterer and in the absence of Mr Leo he really let himself go.

'I love doing your hair, Miss Shore – it's such great hair. Great styles you wear it in on the box, too. I always look for your hair-style, no matter what you're talking about. I mean, even if it's abandoned wives or something heavy like that, I can still enjoy your hair-style, can't I?'

Jemima flashed him one of her famously sweet smiles and sank back under the hood of the dryer.

A while later, she watched, unable to hear with the noise of the dryer, as Mr Leo led Domenica back toward the entrance. As they passed the reception desk, Jemima saw Epiphany mouth something, possibly some words of condolence. In dumb show, Jemima saw Domenica break from her father's grip and shout in the direction of Epiphany.

'*Putana.*' In an Italian opera, that would have been the word, *putana* – prostitute – or something similarly insulting concerning Epiphany's moral character. Whatever the word was, Epiphany did not answer. She dropped her eyes and continued to concentrate on the appointments book in front of her as Mr Leo led his daughter toward the front door.

'I am very sorry to inform you that your appointment is cancelled . . .' The memory of Epiphany's voice came back to Jemima. Could she really have recorded that message so levelly and impersonally after killing her lover?

Yet why had Mr Clark lingered in the salon if not to meet Epiphany? He had certainly taken the trouble to give a false alibi to Domenica, who was expecting her sister-in-law for a late supper. Someone had known he would still be there after hours. Someone had killed him between ten and eleven, when Mr Leo – unnoticed – was still allegedly at the pub and Epiphany was at home – alone.

Jemima closed her eyes. The dryer was getting too hot. Jason, through general enthusiasm no doubt, had a tendency to set the temperature too high. She fiddled with the dial – and in so doing, it occurred to her to wonder under which dryer Mr Clark's corpse had been found sitting. She began, in spite of herself, to imagine the scene. Having been struck – several times, the police said – from behind by the massive metal hair-dryer, Mr Clark had fallen onto the long grey plush seat. The murderer had then propped him up under the plastic hood of one of the dryers to be found when the shop opened in the morning. The killer had left no finger-prints, having – another macabre touch – worn a pair of rubber gloves throughout, no doubt a pair that was missing from the tinting room. The killer had then locked the salon, presumably with Mr Clark's own keys since these too had now vanished.

'At the bottom of the Thames now, no doubt,' Pompey had said dolefully, 'and the gloves along with them.'

Jemima shifted restlessly, sorting images and thoughts in her head. Epiphany's solitary visit to a particularly long-drawn-out film followed by a lonely supper and bed, Mr Leo's alibi. Domenica entertaining her sister-in-law in Clark's absence, Jason's dismissal of abandoned wives – it all began to flow together, to form and re-form in a teasing kaleidoscope.

Where was Jason? She really was getting very hot.

Suddenly Jemima sat upright, hitting her head, rollers and all, on the edge of the hood as she did so. To the surprise of the clients watching (for she still attracted a few curious stares even after several years at Arcangelo's), she lifted the hood, pulled herself to her feet, and strode across the salon to where Epiphany was sitting at the reception desk. Both telephones were for once silent.

'It was true,' said Jemima. 'You *did* go to the cinema and then straight home. Were you angry with him? Had you quarrelled? He waited here for you. But you never came.'

'I told the police that, Miss Shore.' It was anguish, not fear, she had sensed in Epiphany, Jemima realized. 'I told them about the film. Not about the rendezvous. What was the point of telling them about that when I didn't keep it?'

'His appointment was cancelled,' murmured Jemima.

'If only I *had* cancelled it,' Epiphany said. 'Instead, he waited. I pretended I was coming. I wanted him to wait. To suffer as I suffered, waiting for him when he was with her – with her and the baby.' Epiphany's composure broke. 'I could have had any job, but I stayed here like his *slave*, while she held him with her money, the business – '

'I believe you.' Jemima spoke gently. 'And I'm sure the police will, too.'

A short while later, she was explaining it all to Pompey. The policeman, knowing the normally immaculate state of her hair and dress, was somewhat startled to be summoned to a private room at Arcangelo's by a Jemima Shore with her hair still in rollers and her elegant figure draped in a dove-grey Arcangelo's gown.

'I know, I know, Pompey,' she said. 'And for heaven's sake don't tell Mrs Portsmouth you've seen me like this. But the heat of the dryer I was under a few minutes ago gave me an idea. The time of Mr Clark's death was all-important, wasn't it? By heating the body under the dryer and setting the time switch for an hour, the murderer made the police think that he had been killed nearer ten or eleven than the actual seven or eight when he was struck down.

'As it happened, ten or eleven was very awkward for Mr Leo, ostensibly at the pub, but not noticèd in the pub by anyone – I have a feeling that there may be an extra-marital relationship there, too. Mr Leo is still a very good-looking man. That's not our business, however, because Mr Leo didn't kill Mr Clark. Between eight and nine, he was in the Underground on the way home, and there we have many people to vouch for him. As for Epiphany, the girl at the box office verifies that she bought a ticket and the commissionaire that she was in the queue. The timing lets her out, lets them both out, but it lets in someone else – someone who kept the appointment she knew Mr Clark had made. The abandoned wife. Domenica.

'Domenica,' Jemima went on sadly, 'entertaining her sister-in-law from half-past nine onward. Sitting with her, chatting with her. Spending the rest of the long evening with her, pretending to wait for her husband. And all the time he was dead here in the salon. Domenica had worked at the salon – she helped her father build it up. She knew about the rubber gloves and the keys and the hand-dryers and the time switches on the stationary ones.

'Pompey,' Jemima paraphrased Jason: 'it's heavy being an abandoned wife. So in the end, Domenica decided to keep Epiphany's appointment. She even left her baby alone to do so – such was the passion of the woman. The woman scorned. It was she who cancelled all future appointments for Mr Clark, with a heavy blow of a hand-dryer.'

The Girl Who Wanted To See Venice

The furniture in the hotel suite was all on the grand scale, shades of turquoise, painted heavily with gold and upholstered in velvet. Above Jemima Shore's head twinkled an enormous chandelier made of glass drops, with one large central pear, and other swags of diamonds in frozen loops.

Venetian glass, presumably: for this was the Hotel Carpaccio, one of the most lavish (but not modern) hotels looking over the Grand Canal. The flowers – and champagne – sent up by the manager to welcome Jemima Shore Investigator, filming in Venice for Megalith Television, were equally imposing.

At which point, Jemima, gazing at the manager's card, began to laugh. Admittedly Megalith's current series had the overall title 'The British Honeymoon with . . .', Venice forming the subject of the first programme. But that had clearly given Signor Fulco Montevecchi, Hotel Carpaccio, quite the wrong idea, for the card read: 'To wish you all happiness in your married life'. Jemima, being unmarried, and on this occasion on a strictly working trip, was still smiling when there was a soft, persistent rapping on the door.

She imagined the arrival of one of the innumerable deft waiters who had given the Hotel Carpaccio its reputation for luxury and service. Instead she was confronted at the door with a total stranger in the shape of a young man: dark haired, dark eyed, very handsome in an Italianate way, but definitely no waiter.

'Jemima Shore Investigator?' he enquired in an anguished voice. 'It's the police. You've got to persuade them for me. You see, it was all her idea. *She* wanted to see Venice.'

'What on earth – ' began Jemima.

'I'm Harry Hewling,' said the young man; for a moment anguish had given way to puzzlement. He spoke as though the name explained everything.

'I - we're in the next door suite. I've seen you on your balcony. I recognized you. I - we're on our honeymoon.'

'Your flowers! Of course,' cried Jemima, still clutching the card. 'Your wife must have them straightaway.'

The young man gazed at her. 'Don't you understand? Nadia – my wife – has disappeared. And the police seem to think I'm responsible.' He looked down at the Italian newspapers, lying still unopened by the champagne bottle since Jemima's dawn-to-dusk filming routine had not allowed her to read them. Even Jemima's fairly rudimentary Italian was sufficient to translate the glaring headlines: WHERE IS SHE, THE VANISHED ENGLISH BRIDE? IS SHE DEAD, THE BEAUTIFUL ENGLISH HEIRESS?

And for once the story now told by Harry Hewling to Jemima in a series of agitated confidences was certainly bizarre enough to justify such press attention.

Harry and Nadia Hewling had only just got married, in England, having known each other a bare month before that.

'But it was love at first sight,' pressed Harry, in his low desperate voice. 'Love immediately. She was so fantastic. And the reason we got married quickly was *because* of Nadia's loneliness. She'd come from South Africa and her parents were dead. She was alone in the world.'

'And rich?' contributed Jemima gently, thinking of the newspapers.

'Sure she was rich,' exclaimed Harry. 'Nadia happened to inherit a lot of money from a trust fund on her twenty-first birthday. Was that my fault? Sure she paid for everything, including our honeymoon. Sure I'm her husband and I stand to inherit if anything happens to her. Sure she insisted on settling money on me on our marriage – she wanted to make us equal, she said. None of that makes any difference. I keep telling the police: I love her. And she wanted to see Venice.'

'So you definitely weren't marrying her for her money?'

Harry Hewling hesitated, then impulsively took a crumpled photograph out of his pocket. Jemima stared at the slight dark-haired girl feeding the pigeons in the Piazza, St Mark's Byzantine façade in the background.

'Isn't she beautiful? Does a girl like that *need* two hundred thousand pounds to make you fall for her?'

'She's quite lovely.' Jemima thought that together the Hewlings must have made a striking couple, with their regular dark good looks; had she known of their existence in the next-door suite, she might even have interviewed them for 'The British Honeymoon with . . . Venice'. It would have been an amusing twist to interview a real English honeymoon couple on some of the famous locations for what was primarily a cultural investigation.

Jemima stared at the photograph. 'You're quite alike, almost like brother and sister.'

Harry Hewling smiled for the first time. 'Everyone says that. Actually I have got a sister, Gemma, but she's years older than me. She's my half-sister in fact. We're not close.'

But Harry Hewling stopped smiling when he came to the subject of Nadia's disappearance. They'd had a terrific dinner – 'we found this special restaurant in a funny little square off one of the small canals' – and then had walked back to the Carpaccio hand in hand. Up in their suite, Nadia had disappeared into the bedroom and shut the door. That didn't surprise Harry: she would probably re-emerge modelling one of the satin and lace negligées she had brought for the honeymoon. Harry stood for a moment on their balcony looking out over the Grand Canal. It was only after a while, when Nadia had not reappeared, and the door was still closed, that Harry went into their bedroom. But the huge ornate room with its double bed surmounted by a carved eagle, was empty. Harry investigated the marble bathroom. That too was empty.

Somewhat reluctantly he telephoned down to the night porter. It was then that he had his first real surprise. Yes, the Signora Hewling had gone out. She had gone out, out without a coat – but the night was warm – and certainly without luggage. (The police established that by questioning later.)

And from that moment on, there had been no sight or sound of Nadia Hewling, no message, no telephone call. Nothing. She had completely disappeared in Venice, wearing a summer dress and taking with her nothing – nothing, that is, except her passport. In the haste of the wedding, they hadn't had time to change her original passport which was in her maiden name of Nadia Dansk but as Harry said wanly, that had hardly seemed important at the time.

The hotel staff, quite politely, had indicated that there must have been a row and that the Signora would return. Honeymoons did not always go smoothly - even in Venice. At first the Italian police had taken the same line. It was Harry Hewling himself who insisted that there had been no row, insisted they investigate Nadia's disappearance, treat her as a missing person. Now the financial circumstances of Nadia Dansk had come to light, via her English lawyers, the police suddenly turned their attentions to the bridegroom.

Everything began to count against Harry Hewling: the fact that he had been out of work before he met Nadia; the fact that she had made money over to him on marriage; the fact that he would inherit still further funds on her death. And yet in the absence of a body, no corpse having being dredged up from the canal, no unknown body lying in the mortuary, it was difficult for the police to proceed further than interrogating Harry Hewling daily, and suggesting very firmly that he should not leave the city.

'In any case I don't want to leave!' Harry told Jemima. 'Supposing she comes back? She *must* come back.' The airports had been checked, Venice airport first of all, then Milan and the other Italian airports; the railway stations similarly and the various frontiers of the country. No one travelling under the name of Dansk had departed. As for her description – well, a slight dark-haired girl in her twenties with no special characteristics was a common enough sight in Italy at the height of the tourist season.

'And yet she took her passport,' mused Jemima. 'Why does a woman, a pretty young woman on her honeymoon with a wonderful trousseau, take her passport with her unless she intends to travel?' Out of curiosity, or perhaps to give the distraught Harry Hewling the impression she could help him (which she doubted) Jemima allowed herself to be taken next door. She was shown the whole suite. It was in fact identical to her own, except for the rather macabre sight of Nadia Hewling's belongings still hanging in the ornately gilded cupboards, including the Janet Reger-style satin negligées. Then there were her shoes, lots of shiny new high-heeled sandals, totally unworn, still sitting at the bottom of the cupboard.

'What sort of shoes was she wearing when she disappeared?' Jemima asked suddenly, some instinct of feminine curiosity aroused by the sight of this pathetic array of untouched splendour.

'I don't know,' said Harry wretchedly. 'I remember the dress very well because she was wearing it at dinner; turquoise blue, her favourite colour, she changed into it, but the shoes – well, she had so many shoes didn't she?' He pointed. 'How can I remember which pair is missing?'

Jemima thought that whatever pair it was, Nadia Hewling had evidently been very fond of them, considering the fact that Nadia had worn them to travel, throughout her sojourn in Venice, and finally to disappear. Or – a stray thought – did all the beautiful new shoes pinch her? For Venice, Jemima had bought, in a hurry, a pair of shoes one size too small; these shoes, like Nadia's, lay untouched at the bottom of her own

Carpaccio wardrobe. But it was bad luck to make so many bad buys on a honeymoon.

The next day Jemima found that Harry Hewling, in the nicest possible way, was clinging to her company, as though he was still somehow convinced that Jemima Shore would come up with a solution to his problems. His grief and bafflement at his wife's disappearance was so constant and so evident that Jemima did not like to turn him away from her side. She allowed him to accompany her when she was walking towards the Piazza for a cup of coffee, even though she had relished a few days off in solitude, after her filming schedule.

After a while Jemima began to have an uncomfortable feeling that Harry Hewling, for all his recent loss, was finding her, Jemima Shore, increasingly attractive. Then Harry revealed, shyly, that he was an out-of-work actor – and matters became clearer. Presumably he hoped that the magic of Jemima Shore would somehow help to secure him a job in television. . .

They sat outside Florian's, looking at the pigeons and the passers-by together.

'All this,' said Harry Hewling in a broken voice, waving his hand rather wildly in the direction of St Mark's and the Campanile, 'all this was what Nadia wanted to see so much. She wanted to see Venice. And she never did.'

'Except for a very short time,' corrected Jemima.

'*Too* short. Everything about our life together was too short.' There was something about Harry Hewling's generally melodramatic turn of phrase which made Jemima suddenly wonder what kind of actor he was on stage.

Afterwards Jemima could hardly prevent Harry Hewling from walking back with her to the Hotel Carpaccio, although by this time a rather odd train of thought had started in her mind, in spite of herself; a train of thought she really wanted to explore by herself, without the benefit of the company of Harry Hewling, however attractive – for attractive he undeniably was. Jemima was beginning to see exactly how

Nadia Dansk, alone in a strange country, might have fallen unreservedly for Harry.

So Jemima was actually standing with Harry Hewling at the desk as they were asking for their respective keys, when the hotel manager, the generous Sr Fulco Montevecchi, stepped forward, and in his excellent but American-accented English said in a quiet voice:

'Pardon me, Signor Hewling, but would you step this way please?'

The last Jemima saw of Harry Hewling was his back view disappearing, somewhat dwarfed by two rather burly strangers on either side of him. But Jemima Shore was well able to hear Harry Hewling's next utterance, because it was in fact a scream, quite a piercing scream, followed by the noise of someone falling. Jemima, in spite of an instinct which made her want to rush into the manager's office, was obliged to rein in her curiosity and depart – slowly – up the grand staircase which led to her suite. Once there, however, she could hardly settle amid the turquoise and gilded grandeur, the profusion of the manager's scarlet gladioli in honour of a happy married life – which had somehow never been removed – without wondering what had now happened to Harry Hewling. Her curiosity was not gratified for some hours.

Then the figure of Harry Hewling, looking extremely pale and shaken, reappeared at the door of her suite.

'She's dead,' he said in a blank voice. 'Nadia, I mean. I can't believe it. They're saying she drowned herself. They've only just found the body. She must have gone back to England somehow and killed herself. Just like that. I don't believe it. You know, I fainted when I heard the news. Her body has been in the sea all that time and they think it's her . . . the dental records. She did have an English dentist. But of course – ' his voice broke – 'I suppose I shall have to identify her. There's no one else'.

'Your sister – half sister, I mean – '

Harry Hewling looked at Jemima in some surprise.

'You told me you had a sister – '

'On no, you see Gemma never even met Nadia, never even came to the wedding. I told you, we didn't get on.' By now he was openly crying. 'Poor, poor Nadia. I shall *never* understand.'

But Jemima Shore, with a chill feeling, thought that perhaps she did understand, that for the first time she did understand Nadia, the girl who wanted to see Venice, and insisted on coming on her honeymoon, and then left her bridegroom secretly, and flew back to England. Back to England to kill herself. That instinct which nagged at her, leaving her no peace, was telling her that she must somehow go and talk to the detectives who had arrived from England, there must be something they could tell her which would give her the further clue.

'Jemima,' Harry Hewling was saying, 'you will have dinner with me tonight? I suppose I'll have to go back tomorrow, but I would – well, I don't know how to put this, but somehow I'd like to have one evening with you.'

'This has all been a terrible shock,' Jemima replied. 'Why don't you go to your suite? And I'll be in touch with you later.'

It was after a few rapid telephone calls, involving the name of Megalith Television, coupled with that of Jemima Shore, and the mention of little ways in which Jemima Shore had managed to help the police in the past, that Jemima Shore tracked down her quarry. An hour later she was having a drink in the Piazza once more, but this time at Quadri's on the opposite side of the square, with Detective Chief Inspector Ronnie Tree, one of the two detectives who had flown out from England to break the news of Nadia Hewling's death and accompany her husband back to England to identify the body.

'Thank you Jemima, I'll have a campari soda. Make that a double campari soda, while you're at it, if there is such a thing as a double campari soda,' said the Inspector. 'I loathe the stuff, mind you, but I've always wanted to see Venice and frankly it's not worth coming all this way to drink beer, is it? Particularly as we've lost our man.'

'Harry Hewling?' Jemima was drinking Italian white wine

with a great deal more relish than the Inspector was displaying over his campari soda.

'None other. A slippery customer. Oh, a pretty face and all that, I'll grant you he's good looking. If you like the type. As obviously the late Mrs Nadia Hewling did. But it's all too neat, much too neat. And now it seems he's got away with it.'

'Explain –'

'I'd better explain after I've finished this.' The Inspector wrinkled his nose as he drained a huge glass of a red mixture which looked, and evidently tasted to him, like medicine. 'The things I do for England,' he added.

'Yes, I'll explain,' continued the Inspector. 'We had it all made, working with the Italians of course. Bright young man, out-of-work-actor, meets up with shy South African heiress, no relations, seduces her, marries her. She makes a will leaving him everything *and* makes a settlement on him straightaway. The lawyer doesn't like it very much – *he* doesn't like Mr Hewling's pretty face – but there's nothing he can do. Then the wife disappears on honeymoon in Venice, and the husband begins to scream blue murder. Well, it stands to reason, doesn't it? Something very fishy there . . . When she does turn up she's dead as a doornail. And that's where the trouble starts. Mrs Hewling is dead as a doornail in the English sea, and Mr Hewling is alive and well with an unbreakable alibi in the Hotel Carpaccio, Venice. What is more, everyone testifies that he has been there all along; in constant touch with the police. No way he could have followed her and done it.'

'There is a way it could have been done,' said Jemima slowly. 'I'm thinking about some unworn shoes. Masses of shoes: all of them apparently untouched. And a photograph of a dark-haired girl feeding the pigeons in the Piazza. Look, this is what you have to find out . . .'

It was several hours later that Jemima Shore, having returned to her suite, received the call she was expecting.

'Quite right, my dear, quite right,' boomed the voice of Detective Chief Inspector Tree. He sounded remarkably jovial, considering the amount of campari soda he had imbibed; or perhaps it had inspired him. 'How did you guess? The name's Kenyon, by the way, and there's a theatrical background there too. The Italian police will be coming to get him shortly. Murder is an extraditable offence. So how did you guess?'

'First of all, the disappearance of the passport,' said Jemima. 'The point was being made to us: Nadia Hewling was able to travel away from Venice, because she had taken her passport. Yet there was no record of Nadia using the passport to go home: that was odd. Then Harry Hewling impulsively showed me a photograph of a pretty girl – Nadia as he called her – to prove that he had not been fortune-hunting. I pricked his vanity, you see. The first thing I noticed was that it was crumpled, quite old in fact, secondly that it was taken in the Piazza. When I commented that Nadia looked so like him that she might have been his sister, Harry told me very firmly that although he did have a sister, she was much older, and he hardly knew her. He made a point of it. Just as later he insisted that the sister had never met Nadia.'

'Gemma Kenyon,' pronounced Detective Chief Inspector Tree. 'His half-sister, and in fact a few years younger. A would-be actress and much the same type as the wife. In it up to the neck. She travelled out with Hewling on Nadia's own passport under the name of Dansk. Then went home under her own, knowing it was extremely unlikely that anyone would ever trace her, with a different surname, just one of the many dark-haired girls travelling at holiday time. She must have destroyed the Dansk passport en route.'

'But it was the shoes,' pursued Jemima, 'which really made me suspicious. All those totally unused shoes from poor Nadia's trousseau; Gemma must have travelled to Venice and gone out to dinner and left the hotel, all in the same pair. Shoes are very personal things. You can always trust a woman to look at shoes. Gemma could wear Nadia's clothes but not her shoes which were too small. She presumably just brought one pair of her own and wore them all the time. So when Harry

Hewling told me Nadia had never even seen the Piazza, forgetting that rash photograph, then – '

'Then Jemima Shore Investigator became most suspicious,' concluded the Inspector. 'Well, they did for her all right. The pair of them. Did for her in the sea somehow; made sure the body wouldn't be washed up for some time and then went straight off to Venice to give *him* the alibi. We're still working out the details. A pretty pair indeed.'

About twenty minutes later, Jemima was standing on her balcony gazing at the great dome of Santa Maria della Salute across the canal, listening to the evening bells, and thinking that the bells were sounding their own kind of memorial to Nadia Hewling. Then she was aware that Harry Hewling had stepped on to the balcony next door. He was looking at her.

'What are you thinking about, Jemima?' asked Harry. He was smiling. 'Are you thinking about having dinner with me?'

'I'm thinking about a girl who wanted to see Venice,' responded Jemima in a peculiarly expressionless tone, which some at Megalith Television would have recognized as her 'trap' interview voice, when she did not want to arouse the suspicions of her intended victim. 'And never did see it, not even for one day, not even for one day!'

Harry's dark eyes met hers for one instant. For one instant the mask of the actor seemed to drop, the shy young man vanished, to be replaced by some more rapacious kind of animal. He took a step forward, towards her.

Whatever Harry Hewling would have done, Jemima Shore would never know, for at that point she heard a loud knocking at the door of the next-door suite. Harry Hewling continued to look steadily at her.

'You know, you really should not have tried to pick me up as well,' said Jemima. Her voice was now openly hard and cold. 'Otherwise, without a woman's instinct, who knows, you might have actually got away with it.'

Death Of An Old Dog

Paulina Gavin came back from the vet with a sweet expression on her heart-shaped face. The little crease which sometimes – just slightly – marred the smooth white skin between her brows was absent. Her eyes, grey yet soft, swept round the sitting-room. Then they came to rest, lovingly, on Richard.

'Darling, I'm late! But supper won't be late. I've got it all planned.'

Widowhood had made of Richard Gavin a good, as well as a quick, cook. But Paulina had not seen fit to call on his talents before her visit to the vet: he found no note of instructions awaiting him. Now Paulina kissed him with delicious pressure on his cheek, just where his thick grizzled sideburn ended. It was her special place.

From this, Richard knew that Ibo was condemned to die.

Viewing the situation with detachment, as befitting a leading barrister, Richard was not the slightest bit surprised that the verdict should have gone against Ibo. The forces ranged against each other were simply not equal. On the one side, the vet, in his twenties, and Paulina, not much older. On the other side, Ibo. And Ibo was not merely old. He was a very old dog indeed.

He dated from the early days of Richard's first marriage, and that balmy period not only seemed a great while since, a long, long time ago (in the words of Richard's favourite quotation from Ford) but actually was. Even the origin of the nickname Ibo was lost in some private joke of his marriage to Grace: as far as he could remember the dog had begun as Hippolytus. Was it an allusion to his sympathies in the Nigerian Civil War? Based on the fact that Ibo, like the Biafrans, was always starving . . . That too seemed a long, long time ago.

You could therefore say sentimentally that Ibo and Richard had grown old together. Except that it would not actually be true. For Richard had gingerly put out one toe towards middle age, only to be dragged backwards by Paulina's rounded arms, her curiously strong little hands. And having been rescued, Richard was obviously reposited in the prime of life, as though on a throne.

His past athletic prowess (including a really first-class tennis game which only pressure at the Bar had prevented him taking further) was easy to recall, looking at his tall, trim figure. If anything, he had lost weight recently. And it was not only the endearing Pauline but Richard's friends who generally described him as 'handsomer than ever'. It was as though the twenty-five-year age gap between Richard and his second wife had acted upon him as a rejuvenating injection.

The same miracle had not been performed for the master's dog. Casting his mind back, Richard could dimly recall embarrassing walks in the park with Ibo, portrait of a young dog at the evident height of his amorous powers. Now the most desirable spaniel bitch would flaunt herself in vain before him. Like Boxer in *Animal Farm*, where energy was concerned, Ibo was merely a shadow of his former self. And he did not even have Boxer's tragic dignity. Ibo by now was just a very shaggy and, to face the facts fully, a very smelly old dog.

Richard stirred in his chair. The topic must be raised. Besides, he had another important subject to discuss with Paulina, sooner or later.

'How did you get on at the vet's, darling?' he called. She had after all not yet mentioned her visit.

But Paulina, having skipped into her kitchen, apparently did not hear. Pre-arranged odours were wafting from it. Richard guessed that she would soon emerge having removed her apron. He guessed that she would be bearing a bottle of red wine, already opened, and two glasses on a tray. There was, he suspected, a strong possibility that supper would be eaten by candlelight.

Both guesses were correct. The suspicion was confirmed when Paulina artlessly discovered some candles left over from Christmas and decided on impulse to use them up.

'Why not? Just for us,' she enquired to no one in particular, as she sat down at the now positively festive little table with its browny-red casserole, its red Beaujolais and scarlet candles. Then Paulina's manner quite changed.

'Poor Ibo,' sighed Paulina, 'I'm afraid the vet didn't hold out much hope.'

'Hope?' repeated Richard in a surprised voice. It was not surely a question of *hope* – what hope could there possibly be for a very old, very smelly dog – but of life. It was the continuation of Ibo's life they were discussing, for that was all he had to expect, not the possibility of his magical rejuvenation.

'Well, *hope*,' repeated Paulina in her turn, sounding for the first time ruffled, as though the conversation had taken an unexpected and therefore unwelcome turn. 'Hope is so important, isn't it? Without hope, I don't see much point in any of us going on – '

But Richard's attention was distracted. There was an absence. He would have noticed it immediately had it not been for Paulina's charade with the dinner.

Where was Ibo? Obese, waddling, grey muzzled, frequently flea-ridden, half blind, where was Ibo? Normally his first reaction on entering the sitting-room would have been to kiss, no slobber over Richard's hand. Then Ibo, an optimist, might have wagged his stumpy tail as though despite the lateness of the hour and his incapacity, a walk was in the offing. Finally, convinced of his own absurdity, he would have made for the fire, pausing for a last lick of Richard's hand. None of this happened. Where was Ibo?

Paulina began to speak quickly, muttering things about further tests, the young vet's kindness, the need to take a dispassionate decision, and so forth, which all seemed to add up to the fact that the vet had kept the dog in overnight. Once again Richard cut in.

'You do realize Toddie comes home from school to-morrow?'

This time an expression of sheer panic crossed Paulina's face. It was only too obvious she had quite forgotten.

'How can he be?' she began 'He's only just gone there – ' She stopped. She had remembered. Toddie, the strange silent ten-year-old son of Richard's first marriage, was returning the next day from school to have his new plate tightened. The dentist had emphasized that the appointments had to be regular, and had thus overruled protests from Richard who wanted Toddie to wait for half-term. At first Toddie had taken the news of his quick turn round with his usual imperturbability. But after a moment he had suddenly knelt down and flung his arms round Ibo, a mat of fur before the fire.

'Then I'll be seeing you very soon again, won't I, you good old boy? The best dog in the world.' It was a long speech for Toddie.

Toddie's embraces were reserved exclusively for Ibo. His father had tried a few grave kisses after Grace's death. Toddie held himself rigid as though under attack. Later they had settled for ritual handshakes. When Richard married Paulina he had advised her against any form of affectionate assault on Toddie, warned by his own experiences. For Paulina, the frequent light kiss was as natural a mode of communication as Richard's solemn handshake. Baulked of this, she had ended up deprived of any physical contact at all with Toddie. At first it worried her: a motherless boy . . . Later, as her stepson remained taciturn, not so much a motherless boy as an inscrutable person, she was secretly glad she was not committed to hugging and kissing this enigma with his unsmiling lips, and disconcertingly expressionless eyes.

Only two things provoked any kind of visible reaction from Toddie. One was crime, murder to be precise. No doubt it was a natural concomitant to his father's career. But Paulina sometimes found the spectacle of Toddie poring over the newspapers in search of some gruesome trial rather distasteful. It was true that he concentrated on the law reports, showing for example considerable knowledge of appeal procedure, rather than on the horror stories in the popular press. Perhaps he would grow up to be a barrister like Richard . . . In which case, where murder was concerned, he was making a flying start.

Toddie's other visible interest was of course Ibo.

Jolted by the prospect of the boy's return, Paulina now launched into a flood of explanation concerning the true nature of Ibo's condition. Ibo had a large growth, said the vet. Hadn't they noticed it? Richard clenched his hands. How long since he had brought himself to examine Ibo? Ibo simply existed. Or had simply existed up to the present time. Paulina went on to outline the case, extremely lucidly, for 'putting Ibo out of his misery' as she phrased it. Or rather, to be honest, sparing him the misery that was to come. Nobody pretended that Ibo was in violent misery now, a little discomfort perhaps. But he would shortly *be* in misery, that was the point. Richard listened calmly and without surprise. Had he not known since the moment that his wife pressed her lips to his cheek that Ibo was condemned to die?

What Richard Gavin had not realized, and did not realize until he conceded, judicially, regretfully, the case for Ibo's demise, was that the old dog was not actually condemned to die. He was already dead. Had been dead throughout all the fairly long discussion. Had been put to sleep by the vet that very afternoon on the authority, the sole authority, of Paulina Gavin. Who had then returned audaciously, almost flirtatiously, to argue her senior and distinguished husband round to her own point of view . . .

The look on the face of Richard Gavin QC was for one instant quite terrible. But Paulina held up her own quite bravely. With patience – she was not nearly so frightened of Richard now as she had been when they first married – she pointed out to her husband the wisdom and even kindness of her strategy. Someone had to make the decision, and so she, Paulina, had made it. In so doing, she had removed from Richard the hideous, the painful necessity of condemning to death an old friend, a dear old friend. It was easier for her – Richard had after all known Ibo for so much longer. Yet since Richard was such a rational man and loved to think every decision through, she had felt she owed it to him to argue it all out.

'Confident of course that you would make your case?'

Richard's voice sounded guarded, as his voice did sometimes in court, during a cross-examination. His expression was quite blank: for a moment he reminded Paulina uncomfortably of Toddie. But she stuck firmly to her last.

'I know I was right, darling,' she said. 'I acted for the best. You'll see. Someone had to decide.'

There remained the problem of Toddie's precipitate return, the one factor which to be honest, Paulina had left out of her calculations. She had expected to be able to break the sad news at half-term, a decent interval away. But the next morning, Paulina, pretty as a picture in a gingham house-dress at breakfast, made it clear that she could cope with that too. With brightness she handed Richard his mail: '*Personal and Confidential*! Is it the bank?'

With brightness she let it be understood that it was she, Paulina, who would sacrifice her day at the office - the designers' studio she ran with such *élan* – to ferry Toddie to and from school. Although she had already sacrificed an afternoon going to the vet. The only thing Richard was expected to do, Paulina rattled on, was to return from *his* office, in other words his chambers, in the afternoon and tell his son the sad news about the dog.

Richard continued to wear his habitual morning expression, a frown apparently produced by his mail.

'No, it's not the bank,' he said.

'Income Tax, then?' Paulina was determined to make conversation.

'No.'

'Some case, I suppose.'

'You could put it like that.'

'Why here? Why not to your chambers?' Paulina carried on chattily.

'Paulina,' said Richard, pushing back his chair and rising, 'you must understand that I don't exactly look forward to telling Toddie that Ibo is dead.'

'Oh God, darling,' cried Paulina, jumping up in her turn, her eyes starting with bright tears. 'I know, I know, I *know*.' She hugged all that was reachable of his imposing figure. 'But it was for *him*.'

'For Ibo?'

'Yes, for him. That poor dear old fellow. Poor, poor old Ibo. I know, I understand. It's the saddest thing in the world, the death of an old dog. But it is – somehow – isn't it, darling, inevitable?'

The hugging came to an end, and then Paulina dried her tears. Richard went off to his study, the large book-lined room which Paulina had created for him above the garage. He indicated that he would telephone his clerk with a view to taking the whole day off from his chambers.

One of the features of the study was a large picture window which faced out at the back over the fields to the wood. To protect Richard's privacy, the study had no windows overlooking the house. There was merely a brick façade. This morning, Paulina suddenly felt that both the study and Richard were turning their back on her. But that was fanciful. She was overwrought on account of poor Toddie. And of course poor Ibo.

Paulina reminded herself that she too was not without her feelings, her own fondness for the wretched animal. It had been a brave and resolute thing she had done to spare Richard, something of which she would not have been capable of a few years back. How much the studio had done for her self-confidence! Nerves calmed by the contemplation of her new wise maturity, Paulina got the car out of the garage and went off to fetch Toddie.

Of course Toddie knew something was wrong the moment he entered the empty house. He slipped out of the car and ran across the courtyard the moment they returned; although by re-parking the car in the garage immediately, Paulina hoped to propel him straight into his father's care. As it was, she refused to answer Toddie's agitated question as to why Ibo did not come to greet him. She simply took him by the shoulder and led him back as fast as possible to the garage. Then it was up the stairs and into the study. Paulina did not intend to linger. She had no wish to witness the moment of Toddie's breakdown.

She had once asked Richard how Toddie took the news of his mother's death, so sudden, so appalling, in a road accident on the way to pick him up at kindergarten.

'He howled,' Richard replied.

'You mean, cried and cried.'

'No, howled. Howled once. One terrible howl, then nothing. Just as if someone had put their hand across his mouth to stop him. It was a howl like a dog.'

Paulina shuddered. It was a most distasteful comparison to recall at the present moment. She was by now at the head of the narrow staircase and thrusting Toddie into the big book-lined room with its vast window. But before she could leave, Richard was saying in that firm voice she recognized from the courts: 'Toddie, you know about the law, don't you?'

The boy nodded and stared.

'Well, I want you to know that there has been a trial here. The trial of Ibo.' Toddie continued to stare, his large round eyes almost fish-like. Paulina turned and fled away down the stairs. No doubt Richard knew his own business – and his own son – best. But to her it sounded a most ghoulish way of breaking the news.

A great deal of time passed; time enough for Paulina to speak several times to her office (pleasingly incapable of managing without her); time enough for Paulina to reflect how very unused she had become to a housewife's enforced idleness, waiting on the movements of the males of the family. She tried to fill the gap by making an interesting tea for Toddie, in case that might solace him. But it was in fact long past tea-time when Paulina finally received some signal from the study across the way. She was just thinking that if Richard did not emerge soon, she would be late returning Toddie to Greybanks (and that would hardly help him to recover) when the bleep-bleep of the intercom roused her.

'He's coming down,' said Richard's voice, slightly distorted by the wire which crackled. 'Naturally he doesn't want to talk about it. So would you take him straight back to school? As soon as possible. No, no tea thank you. He'll be waiting for you in the car.' And that was all. The intercom clicked off.

Upset, in spite of herself, by Richard's brusqueness, Paulina hastily put away the interesting tea as best she could. Still fighting down her feelings, she hurried to put on her jacket and re-cross the courtyard. But she could not quite extinguish all resentment. It was lucky, she thought crossly, that as Richard grew older he would have a tactful young wife at his elbow; that should preserve him from those slight rigidities, or perhaps acidities was a better word, to which all successful men were prone after a certain age. For the second time that day she recalled with satisfaction the moral courage she had shown in having Ibo put down on her own initiative without distressing her husband; there was no doubt that Richard was relying on her already.

This consciousness of virtue enabled her – but only just – to stifle her irritation at the fact that Richard had not even bothered to open the big garage doors for her. Really, men were the most ungrateful creatures; it was she, not Richard, who was facing a cross-country journey in the dark; he might at least have shown his normal chivalry to ease her on her way – taking back his son, not hers, to school. Reliance was one thing, dependence and over-dependence quite another. Still in an oddly perturbed mood for one normally so calm and competent, Paulina slipped through the little door which led to the garage.

She went towards the car. She was surprised that the engine was already running. And Toddie was not in the passenger seat. In fact the car appeared to be empty. She tried the door. It was locked. Behind her came the noise of the little side-door shutting.

About the same time Richard Gavin was thinking that he would miss Paulina, he really would: her cooking, her pretty ways, her office gossip. Habit had even reconciled him to the latter. In many ways she had been a delightful, even a delicious, wife for a successful man. The trouble was that she clearly would not make any sort of wife for an older man dying slowly and probably painfully of an incurable disease. This morning the doctors had finally given him no hope. He had been waiting for the last hope to vanish, putting off the moment, before sharing the fearful burden with her.

Really her ruthless and overbearing behaviour over poor Ibo had been a blessing in disguise. For it had opened his eyes just in time. No, Paulina would certainly not be the kind of wife to solace her husband's protracted deathbed. She might even prove to be the dreadful sort of person who believed in euthanasia 'to put him out of his misery'. He corrected himself. Paulina might even *have* proved to be such a person.

Back in the garage, the smell of exhaust fumes soon began to fill the air. Still no one came to open the garage doors. Even the side-door was now apparently locked from the outside. Paulina's last conscious thought, fighting in vain to get the garage doors open, was that she would really have to arrange automatic openers one of these days – now that Richard was no longer as young as he was, no longer eager to help her.

A couple of fields away, in a copse, Toddie was showing his father the exact spot where he would like to have Ibo buried. Richard had been quite desperate, as he would tell the police later, to cheer the poor little chap up. It was a natural, if sentimental expedition for a father to make with his son. A son so bereft by the death of an old dog. A son so early traumatized by the death of his mother (a step-mother was not at all the same thing, alas).

And when the police came, as they surely would, to the regrettable conclusion that the second Mrs Gavin's death had not in fact been an accident, well, it really all added up, didn't it? Exactly the same factors came into play and would be ably, amply, interminably examined by the long lists of child psychiatrists to whom Toddie would be inevitably subjected.

But Toddie, Richard reflected with a certain professional detachment, would be more than a match for them. What interested him most about his son was his burning desire to get on with the business of confessing his crime. He seemed to be positively looking forward to his involvement with the police and so forth. He was certainly very satisfied with the way he had compassed his step-mother's death.

Richard was also quite surprised at the extent of Toddie's knowledge of the law concerning murderers. You could almost say that Toddie had specialized in the subject. Whereas he himself had never had much to do with that line of country. Richard realized suddenly that it was the first time he had ever really felt interested in his son.

Under the circumstances, Toddie very much doubted that he would have to spend many years in prison. He intended to end up as a model prisoner. But there might have to be a bad patch from which he could be redeemed: otherwise he might not present an interesting enough case, and the interesting cases always got out first. No, Toddie really had it all worked out.

'Besides, Dad,' ended Toddie, no longer in the slightest bit taciturn, 'I'm proud of what I did. You told me how to do it.

But I'd have done it somehow anyway. She deserved to die. She condemned Ibo to death without telling us. Behind our backs. No proper trial. And killed him. Ibo, the best dog in the world.'

Have A Nice Death

Everyone was being extraordinarily courteous to Sammy Luke in New York.

Take Sammy's arrival at Kennedy Airport, for example: Sammy had been quite struck by the warmth of the welcome. Sammy thought: how relieved Zara would be! Zara (his wife) was inclined to worry about Sammy – he had to admit, with some cause; in the past, that is. In the past Sammy had been nervous, delicate, highly strung, whatever you liked to call it – Sammy suspected that some of Zara's women friends had a harsher name for it; the fact was that things tended to go wrong where Sammy was concerned, unless Zara was there to iron them out. But that was in England. Sammy was quite sure he was not going to be nervous in America; perhaps, cured by the New World, he would never be nervous again.

Take the immigration officials – hadn't Sammy been warned about them?

'They're nothing but gorillas' – Zara's friend, wealthy Tess, who travelled frequently to the States, had pronounced the word in a dark voice. For an instant Sammy, still in his nervous English state, visualized immigration checkpoints manned by terrorists armed with machine-guns. But the official seated in a booth, who summoned Sammy in, was slightly built, perhaps even slighter than Sammy himself though the protection of the booth made it difficult to tell.

And he was smiling as he cried:

'C'mon, c'mon, bring the family!' A notice outside the booth stated that only one person – or one family – was permitted inside at a time.

'I'm afraid my wife's not travelling with me,' stated Sammy apologetically.

'I sure wish my wife wasn't with me either,' answered the official, with ever increasing bonhomie.

Sammy wondered confusedly – it had been a long flight after all – whether he should explain his own very different feelings about his wife, his passionate regret that Zara had not been able to accompany him. But his new friend was already examining his passport, flipping through a large black directory, talking again: 'A writer . . . Would I know any of your books?'

This was an opportunity for Sammy to explain intelligently the purpose of his visit. Sammy Luke was the author of six novels. Five of them had sold well, if not astoundingly well, in England and not at all in the United States. The sixth, *Women Weeping*, due perhaps to its macabrely fashionable subject-matter, had hit some kind of publishing jackpot in both countries. Only a few weeks after publication in the States, its sales were phenomenal and rising; an option on the film rights (maybe Jane Fonda and Meryl Streep as the masochists?) had already been bought. As a result of all this, Sammy's new American publishers believed hotly that only one further thing was necessary to ensure the vast, the *total* success of *Women Weeping* in the States, and that was to make of its author a television celebrity. Earnestly defending his own position on the subject of violence and female masochism on a series of television interviews and talk shows, Sammy Luke was expected to shoot *Women Weeping* high high into the best-seller lists and keep it there. All this was the firm conviction of Sammy's editor at Porlock Publishers, Clodagh Jansen.

'You'll be great on the talk shows, Sammy,' Clodagh had cawed down the line from the States – 'So little and cute and then – ' Clodagh made a loud noise with her lips as if someone was gobbling someone else up. Presumably it was not Sammy who was to be gobbled. Clodagh was a committed feminist, as she had carefully explained to Sammy on her visit to England, when she had bought *Women Weeping*, against much competition, for a huge sum. But she believed in the social role of best-sellers like *Women Weeping* to finance radical feminist works. Sammy had tried to explain that his book was in no way anti-feminist, no way at all, witness the fact that Zara herself, his Egeria, had not complained –

'Save it for the talk shows, Sammy,' was all that Clodagh had replied.

While Sammy was still wondering how to put all this concisely, but to his best advantage, at Kennedy Airport, the man in the booth asked: 'And the purpose of your visit, Mr Luke?'

Sammy was suddenly aware that he had drunk a great deal on the long flight – courtesy of Porlock's first-class ticket – and slept too heavily as well. His head began to sing. But whatever answer he gave, it was apparently satisfactory. The man stamped the white sheet inside his passport and handed it back. Then: 'Enjoy your visit to the United States of America, Mr Luke. Have a nice day now.'

'Oh, I will, I know I will,' promised Sammy. 'It seems a lovely day here already.'

Sammy's experiences at the famous Barraclough Hotel (accommodation arranged by Clodagh) were if anything even more heart-warming. Everyone, but everyone, at the Barraclough wanted Sammy to enjoy himself during his visit.

'Have a nice day, now Mr Luke': most conversations ended like that, whether they were with the hotel telephonist, the agreeable men who operated the lifts or the gentlemanly *concierge*. Even the New York taxi-drivers, from whose guarded expressions Sammy would not otherwise have suspected such warm hearts, wanted Sammy to have a nice day.

'Oh, I will, I will,' Sammy began by answering. After a bit

he added: 'I just adore New York,' said with a grin and the very suspicion of an American twang.

'This is the friendliest city in the world,' he told Zara down the long-distance telephone, shouting, so that his words were accompanied by little vibratory echoes.

'Tess says they don't really mean it.' Zara's voice in contrast was thin, diminished into a tiny wail by the line. 'They're not sincere, you know.'

'Tess was wrong about the gorillas at Immigration. She could be wrong about that too. Tess doesn't *own* the whole country you know. She just inherited a small slice of it.'

'Darling, you do sound funny,' countered Zara; her familiar anxiety on the subject of Sammy made her sound stronger. 'Are you all right? I mean, are you all right over there all by yourself – '

'I'm mainly on television during the day,' Sammy cut in with a laugh. 'Alone except for the chat-show host and forty million people.' Sammy was deciding whether to add, truthfully, that actually not all the shows were networked; some of his audiences being as low as a million, or say a million and a half, when he realized that Zara was saying in a voice of distinct reproach:

'And you haven't asked after Mummy yet.' It was the sudden illness of Zara's mother, another person emotionally dependent upon her, which had prevented Zara's trip to New York with Sammy, at the last moment.

It was only after Sammy had rung off – having asked tenderly after Zara's mother and apologized for his crude crack about Tess before doing so – that he realized Zara was quite right. He *had* sounded rather funny: even to himself. That is, he would never have dared to make such a remark about Tess in London. Dared? Sammy pulled himself up.

To Zara, his strong and lovely Zara, he could of course say anything. She was his wife. As a couple, they were exceptionally close as all their circle agreed; being childless (a decision begun through poverty in the early days and somehow never rescinded) only increased their intimacy.

Because their marriage had not been founded on a flash-in-the-pan sexual attraction but something deeper, more companionate – sex had never played a great part in it, even at the beginning – the bond had only grown stronger with the years. Sammy doubted whether there was a more genuinely united pair in London.

All this was true; and comforting to recollect. It was just that in recent years Tess had become an omnipresent force in their lives: Tess on clothes, Tess on interior decoration, especially Tess on curtains, that was the real pits – a new expression which Sammy had picked up from Clodagh; and somehow Tess's famous money always seemed to reinforce her opinions in a way which was rather curious, considering Zara's own radical contempt for unearned wealth.

'Well I've got money now. Lots and lots of it. Earned money,' thought Sammy, squaring his thin shoulders in the new pale-blue jacket which Zara, yes Zara, had made him buy. He looked in one of the huge gilded mirrors which decorated his suite at the Barraclough, pushing aside the large floral arrangement, a gift from the hotel manager (or was it Clodagh?) to do so. Sammy Luke, the conqueror of New York or at least American television; then he had to laugh at his own absurdity.

He went on to the little balcony which led off the suite's sitting-room and looked down at the ribbon of streets which stretched below; the roofs of lesser buildings; the blur of green where Central Park nestled, at his disposal, in the centre of it all. The plain truth was that he was just very very happy. The reason was not purely the success of his book, nor even his instant highly commercial fame, as predicted by Clodagh, on television, nor yet the attentions of the Press, parts of which had after all been quite violently critical of his book, again as predicted by Clodagh. The reason was that Sammy Luke felt loved in New York in a vast wonderful impersonal way. Nothing was demanded of him by this love; it was like an electric fire which simulated red-hot coals even when it was switched off. New York glowed but it could not scorch. In his heart Sammy knew that he had never been so happy before.

It was at this point that the telephone rang again. Sammy left the balcony. Sammy was expecting one of three calls. The first, and most likely, was Clodagh's daily checking call: 'Hi, Sammy, it's Clodagh Pegoda . . . listen, that show was great, the one they taped. Our publicity girl actually told me it didn't go too well at the time, she was frightened they were mauling you . . . but the way it came out . . . Zouch!' More interesting sounds from Clodagh's mobile and rather sensual lips. 'That's my Sam. You really had them licked. I guess the little girl was just over-protective. Sue-May, was it? Joanie. Yes, Joanie. She's crazy about you. I'll have to talk to her; what's a nice girl like that doing being crazy about a man, and a married man at that . . . '

Clodagh's physical preference for her own sex was a robust joke between them; it was odd how being in New York made that too seem innocuous. In England Sammy had been secretly rather shocked by the frankness of Clodagh's allusions: more alarmingly she had once goosed him, apparently fooling, but with the accompanying words, 'You're a bit like a girl yourself, Sammy', which were not totally reassuring. Even that was preferable to the embarrassing occasion when Clodagh had playfully declared a physical attraction to Zara, wondered – outside the money that was now coming in – how Zara put up with Sammy. In New York however Sammy entered enthusiastically into the fun.

He was also pleased to hear, however lightly meant, that Joanie, the publicity girl in charge of his day-to-day arrangements, was crazy about him; for Joanie, unlike handsome piratical frightening Clodagh, was small and tender.

The second possibility for the call was Joanie herself. In which case she would be down in the lobby of the Barraclough, ready to escort him to an afternoon taping at a television studio across town. Later Joanie would drop Sammy back at the Barraclough, paying carefully and slightly earnestly for the taxi as though Sammy's nerves might be ruffled if the ceremony was not carried out correctly. One of these days, Sammy thought with a smile, he might even ask Joanie up to his suite at the Barraclough . . . after all what were suites for? (Sammy had never had a suite in a hotel before, his English publisher having an old-fashioned taste for providing his authors with plain bedrooms while on promotional tours.)

The third possibility was that Zara was calling him back: their conversation, for all Sammy's apologies, had not really ended on a satisfactory note; alone in London, Zara was doubtless feeling anxious about Sammy as a result. He detected a little complacency in himself about Zara: after all, there was for once nothing for her to feel anxious about (except perhaps Joanie, he added to himself with a smile).

Sammy's complacency was shattered by the voice on the telephone: 'I saw you on television last night,' began the voice – female, whispering. 'You bastard, Sammy Luke, I'm coming up to your room and I'm going to cut off your little – ' A detailed anatomical description followed of what the voice was going to do to Sammy Luke. The low violent obscenities, so horrible, so surprising, coming out of the innocent white hotel telephone, continued for a while unstopped, assaulting his ears like the rustle of some appalling cowrie shell; until Sammy thought to clutch the instrument to his chest, and thus stifle the voice in the surface of his new blue jacket.

After a moment, thinking he might have put an end to the terrible whispering, Sammy raised the instrument again. He was in time to hear the voice say: 'Have a nice death, Mr. Luke.'

Then there was silence.

Sammy felt quite sick. A moment later he was running across the ornate sitting-room of the splended Barraclough suite, retching; the bathroom seemed miles away at the far end of the spacious bedroom; he only just reached it in time.

Sammy was lying, panting, on the nearest twin bed to the door – the one which had been meant for Zara – when the telephone rang again. He picked it up and held it at a distance, then recognized the merry interested voice of the hotel telephonist.

'Oh, Mr Luke,' she was saying. 'While your line was busy just now Joanie Lazlo called from Porlock Publishers, and she'll call right back. But she says to tell you that the taping for this afternoon has been cancelled. Max Syegrand is still tied up on the Coast and can't make it. Too bad about that, Mr Luke. It's a good show. Anyway, she'll come by this evening with some more books to sign . . . Have a nice day now, Mr Luke.' And the merry telephonist rang off. But this time Sammy shuddered when he heard the familiar cheerful farewell.

It seemed a long time before Joanie rang to say that she was downstairs in the hotel lobby, and should she bring the copies of *Women Weeping* up to the suite? When she arrived at the sitting-room door, carrying a Mexican tote bag weighed down by books, Joanie's pretty little pink face was glowing and she gave Sammy her usual softly enthusiastic welcome. All the same Sammy could hardly believe that he had contemplated seducing her – or indeed anyone – in his gilded suite amid the floral arrangements. That all seemed a very long while ago.

For in the hours before Joanie's arrival, Sammy received two more calls. The whispering voice grew bolder still in its description of Sammy's fate; but it did not grow stronger. For some reason, Sammy listened to the first call through to the end. At last the phrase came: although he was half expecting it, his heart still thumped when he heard the words: 'Have a nice death now, Mr Luke.'

With the second call, he slammed down the telephone immediately and then called back the operator: 'No more,' he said loudly and rather breathlessly. 'No more, I don't want any more.'

'Pardon me, Mr Luke?'

'I meant, I don't want any more calls, not like that, not now.'

'Alrighty.' The operator – it was another voice, not the merry woman who habitually watched television, but just as friendly. 'I'll hold your calls for now, Mr Luke. I'll be happy to do it. Goodbye now. Have a nice evening.'

Should Sammy perhaps have questioned this new operator about his recent caller? No doubt she would declare herself happy to discuss the matter. But he dreaded a further cheerful impersonal New York encounter in his shaken state. Besides, the first call had been put through by the merry television-watcher. Zara. He needed to talk to Zara. She would know what to do; or rather she would know what *he* should do.

'What's going on?' she exclaimed. 'I tried to ring you three times and that bloody woman on the hotel switchboard wouldn't put me through. Are you all right? I rang you back because you sounded so peculiar. Sort of high, you were laughing at things, things which weren't really funny, it's not like you, is it, in New York people are supposed to get this energy, but I never thought – '

'I'm not all right, not all right at all,' Sammy interrupted her; he was aware of a high rather tremulous note in his voice. 'I was all right then, more than all right, but now I'm not, not at all.' Zara couldn't at first grasp what Sammy was telling her, and in the end he had to abandon all explanations of his previous state of exhilaration. For one thing Zara couldn't seem to grasp what he was saying, and for another Sammy was guiltily aware that absence from Zara's side had played more than a little part in this temporary madness. So Sammy settled for agreeing that he had been acting rather oddly since he had arrived in New York, and then appealed to Zara to advise him how next to proceed.

Once Sammy had made this admission, Zara sounded more like her normal brisk but caring self. She told Sammy to ring up Clodagh at Porlock.

'Frankly, Sammy, I can't think why you didn't ring her straight away.' Zara pointed out that if Sammy could not, Clodagh certainly could and would deal with the hotel switchboard, so that calls were filtered, the lawful distinguished from the unlawful.

'Clodagh might even know the woman,' observed Sammy weakly at one point. 'She has some very odd friends.'

Zara laughed. 'Not *that* odd, I hope.' Altogether she was in a better temper. Sammy remembered to ask after Zara's mother before he rang off; and on hearing that Tess had flown to America on business, he went so far as to say that he would love to have a drink with her.

When Joanie arrived in the suite, Sammy told her about the threatening calls and was vaguely gratified by her distress.

'I think that's just dreadful, Sammy,' she murmured, her light hazel eyes swimming with some tender emotion. 'Clodagh's not in the office right now, but let me talk with the hotel manager right away . . .' Yet it was odd how Joanie no longer seemed in the slightest bit attractive to Sammy. There was even something cloying about her friendliness; perhaps there was a shallowness there, a surface brightness concealing nothing; perhaps Tess was right and New Yorkers were after all insincere. All in all, Sammy was pleased to see Joanie depart with the signed books.

He did not offer her a second drink, although she had brought him an advance copy of the *New York Times* book section for Sunday, showing that *Women Weeping* had jumped four places in the best-seller list.

'Have a nice evening, Sammy,' said Joanie softly as she closed the door of the suite. 'I've left a message with Clodagh's answering service and I'll call you tomorrow.'

But Sammy did not have a very nice evening. Foolishly he decided to have dinner in his suite; the reason was that he had some idiotic lurking fear that the woman with the whispering voice would be lying in wait for him outside the Barraclough.

'Have a nice day,' said the waiter automatically who delivered the meal on a heated trolley covered in a white damask cloth, after Sammy had signed the chit. Sammy hated him.

'The day is over. It is evening.' Sammy spoke in a voice which was pointed, almost vicious; he had just deposited a tip on the white chit.

By this time the waiter, stowing the dollars rapidly and expertly in his pocket was already on his way to the door; he turned and flashed a quick smile: 'Yeah. Sure. Thank you, Mr Luke. Have a nice day.' The waiter's hand was on the door handle.

'It is evening here!' exclaimed Sammy. He found he was shaking. 'Do you understand? Do you agree that it is *evening*?' The man, mildly startled, but not at all discomposed, said again: 'Yeah. Sure. Evening. Goodbye now.' And he went.

Sammy poured himself a whisky from the suite's mini-bar. He no longer felt hungry. The vast white expanse of his dinner trolley depressed him, because it reminded him of his encounter with the waiter; at the same time he lacked the courage to push the trolley boldly out of the suite into the corridor. Having avoided leaving the Barraclough he now found that even more foolishly he did not care to open the door of his own suite.

Clodagh being out of the office, it was doubtless Joanie's fault that the hotel operators still ignored their instructions. Another whispering call was let through, about ten o'clock at night, as Sammy was watching a movie starring the young Elizabeth Taylor, much cut up by commercials, on television. (If he stayed awake till midnight, he could see himself on one of the talk shows he had recorded.) The operator was now supposed to announce the name of each caller, for Sammy's inspection; but this call came straight through.

There was a nasty new urgency in what the voice was promising: 'Have a nice death now. I'll be coming by quite soon, Sammy Luke.'

In spite of the whisky – he drained yet another of the tiny bottles – Sammy was still shaking when he called down to the operator and protested: 'I'm still getting these calls. You've got to do something. You're supposed to be keeping them away from me.'

The operator, not a voice he recognized, sounded rather puzzled, but full of goodwill; spurious goodwill, Sammy now felt. Even if she was sincere, she was certainly stupid. She did not seem to recall having put through anyone to Sammy within the last ten minutes. Sammy did not dare instruct her to hold all calls in case Zara rang up again (or Clodagh, for that matter; where was Clodagh, now that he needed protection from this kind of feminist nut?). He felt too desperate to cut himself off altogether from contact with the outside world. What would Zara advise?

The answer was really quite simple, once it had occurred to him. Sammy rang down to the front desk and complained to the house manager who was on night duty. The house manager, like the operator, was rather puzzled, but extremely polite.

'Threats, Mr Luke? I assure you you'll be very secure at the Barraclough. We have guards naturally, and we are accustomed . . . but if you'd like me to come up to discuss the matter, why I'd be happy to . . . '

When the house manager arrived, he was quite charming. He referred not only to Sammy's appearance on television but to his actual book. He told Sammy he'd loved the book; what was more he'd given another copy to his eighty-three-year-old mother (who'd seen Sammy on the Today show) and she'd loved it too. Sammy was too weary to wonder more than passingly what an eighty-three-year-old mother would make of *Women Weeping*. He was further depressed by the house manager's elaborate courtesy; it wasn't absolutely clear whether he believed Sammy's story, or merely thought he was suffering from the delightful strain of being a celebrity. Maybe the guests at the Barraclough behaved like that all the time, describing imaginary death threats? That possibility also Sammy was too exhausted to explore.

At midnight he turned the television on again and watched himself, on the chat show in the blue jacket, laughing and wriggling with his own humour, denying for the tenth time that he had any curious sadistic tastes himself, that *Women Weeping* was founded on an incident in his private life.

When the telephone rang sharply into the silence of the suite shortly after the end of the show, Sammy knew that it would be his persecutor; nevertheless the sight of his erstwhile New York self, so debonair so confident, had given him back some strength. Sammy was no longer shaking as he picked up the receiver.

It was Clodagh on the other end of the line, who had just returned to New York from somewhere out of town and picked up Joanie's message from her answering service. Clodagh listened carefully to what Sammy had to say and answered him with something less than her usual loud-hailing zest.

'I'm not too happy about this one,' she said after what – for Clodagh – was quite a lengthy silence. 'Ever since Andy Warhol, we can never be quite sure what these jokers will do. Maybe a press release tomorrow? Sort of protect you with publicity *and* sell a few more copies. Maybe not. I'll think about that one, I'll call Joanie in the morning.' To Sammy's relief, Clodagh was in charge.

There was another pause. When Clodagh spoke again, her tone was kindly, almost maternal; she reminded him, surprisingly, of Zara.

'Listen, little Sammy, stay right there and I'll be over. We don't want to lose an author, do we?'

Sammy went on to the little balcony which led off the sitting-room and gazed down at the street-lights far far below; he did not gaze too long, partly because Sammy suffered from vertigo (although that had become much better in New York) and partly because he wondered whether an enemy was waiting for him down below. Sammy no longer thought all the lights were twinkling with goodwill. Looking downward he imagined Clodagh, a strong Zara-substitute, striding towards him to save him.

When Clodagh did arrive, rather suddenly, at the door of the suite – maybe she did not want to alarm him by telephoning up from the lobby of the hotel? – she did look very strong, as well as handsome, in her black designer jeans and black silk shirt; through her shirt he could see the shape of her flat muscular chest, with the nipples clearly defined, like the chest of a young Greek athlete.

'Little Sammy,' said Clodagh quite tenderly. 'Who would want to frighten you?'

The balcony windows were still open. Clodagh made Sammy pour himself yet another whisky and one for her too (there was a trace of the old Clodagh in the acerbity with which she gave these orders). Masterfully she also imposed two mysterious bomb-like pills upon Sammy which she promised, together with the whisky, would give him sweet dreams 'and no nasty calls to frighten you'.

Because Clodagh was showing a tendency to stand very close to him, one of her long arms affectionately and irremoveably round his shoulders, Sammy was not all that unhappy when Clodagh ordered him to take both their drinks on to the balcony, away from the slightly worrying intimacy of the suite.

Sammy stood at the edge of the parapet, holding both glasses, and looked downwards. He felt better. Some of his previous benevolence towards New York came flooding back as the whisky and pills began to take effect. Sammy no longer imagined that his enemy was down there in the street outside the Barraclough, waiting for him.

In a way of course, Sammy was quite right. For Sammy's enemy was not down there in the street below, but standing silently right there behind him, on the balcony, black gloves on her big capable strong hands where they extended from the cuffs of her chic black silk shirt.

'Have a nice death now, Sammy Luke.' Even the familiar phrase hardly had time to strike a chill into his heart as Sammy found himself falling, falling into the deep trough of the New York street twenty-three stories below. The two whisky glasses flew from his hands and little icy glass fragments scattered far and wide, far far from Sammy's tiny slumped body where it hit the pavement; the whisky vanished altogether, for no one recorded drops of whisky falling on their face in Madison Avenue.

Soft-hearted Joanie cried when the police showed her Sammy's typewritten suicide note with that signature so familiar from the signing of the books; the text itself the last product of the battered portable typewriter Sammy had brought with him to New York. But Joanie had to confirm Sammy's distressed state at her last visit to the suite; an impression more than confirmed by the amount of whisky Sammy had consumed before his death – a glass in each hand as he fell, said the police – to say nothing of the pills.

The waiter contributed to the picture too.

'I guess the guy seemed quite upset when I brought him his dinner.' He added as an afterthought: 'He was pretty lonesome too. Wanted to talk. You know the sort. Tried to stop me going away. Wanted to have a conversation. I should'a stopped but I was busy.' The waiter was genuinely regretful.

The hotel manager was regretful too, which considering the fact that Sammy's death had been duly reported in the Press as occurring from a Barraclough balcony, was decent of him.

One of the operators – Sammy's merry friend – went further and was dreadfully distressed: 'Jesus, I don't believe it. For Christ's sake, I just saw him on television.' The other operator made a calmer statement simply saying that Sammy had seemed very indecisive about whether he wished to receive calls or not in the course of the evening.

Zara Luke, in England, told the story of Sammy's last day and his pathetic tales of persecution, not otherwise substantiated. She also revealed – not totally to the surprise of her friends – that Sammy had a secret history of mental breakdown and was particularly scared of travelling by himself.

'I shall always blame myself for letting him go,' ended Zara, brokenly.

Clodagh Jansen of Porlock Publishers made a dignified statement about the tragedy.

It was Clodagh too who met the author's widow at the airport when Zara flew out a week later to make all the dreadful arrangements consequent upon poor Sammy's death.

At the airport Clodagh and Zara embraced discreetly, tearfully. It was only in private later at Clodagh's apartment – for Zara to stay at the Barraclough would certainly have been totally inappropriate – that more intimate caresses of a richer quality began. Began, but did not end: neither had any reason to hurry things.

'After all, we've all the time in the world,' murmured Sammy's widow to Sammy's publisher.

'And all the money too,' Clodagh whispered back; she must remember to tell Zara that *Women Weeping* would reach the Number One spot in the best-seller list on Sunday.

Boots

Her mother used to call her Little Red Riding Boots, and eventually by degrees of use (and affection) just Boots. And now that Emily was no longer quite so little – the smart red plastic boots which had given rise to the joke, were beginning to pinch – she still liked being called the pet name by her mother. It was a private matter between them.

Emily's mother, Cora, was a widow: a pretty slight young woman, not yet thirty, but still a widow. When Emily was a baby, her father had gone away to somewhere hot on an engineering project and got himself killed. That at least was how Emily had heard Cora describing the situation on the occasion of her first date with Mr Inch.

'And not a penny after all these years,' Cora added. 'Just a load of luggage months later. Including the clothes he was *wearing*! Still covered in his blood . . . '

Then Mr Inch – not Cora – got up and shut the door.

Listening from her little bedroom, which was just next to the sitting-room, Emily imagined her father getting himself killed. Or rather she thought of the nasty accident she had recently witnessed on the zebra crossing opposite their house. Blood everywhere. Rather as if the old woman had been exploded, like you sometimes saw on the news on television. The old woman had been hit by one of the nasty long lorries which were always rumbling down their particular high street. Cora felt very strongly about the lorries, and often spoke to Emily about them, complaining about them, warning her about the crossing.

Perhaps that was why Cora had let Emily go on watching the scene out of the window when the old woman was hit, for quite a long time, in spite of all the blood.

Later Cora explained her views on this kind of thing to Mr Inch and Emily listened.

'You see, you can't protect a child from life. From the first I never hid anything from Boots – Emily. It's all around us, isn't it? I mean, I want Emily to grow up knowing all about life: that's the best kind of protection, isn't it?'

'She is awfully young.' Mr Inch sounded rather doubtful. 'Perhaps it's just because she looks so tiny and delicate. Such a little doll. And pretty too. One wants to protect her. Pretty like her mother – '

On this occasion also, Mr Inch got up and shut the door. He was always shutting the door, thought Emily, shutting her out as if he did not like her. And yet when Mr Inch was alone with her, if her mother was cooking something smelly with the door shut, even more if Cora dashed down to the shops, Mr Inch used to take the opportunity to say that he liked Emily, that he liked Emily very much. And perhaps one day, who could say, perhaps Mr Inch might come to live with Emily and her mother all the time – would Emily like that?

At this point Mr Inch generally touched Emily's long thick curly hair, not gold but brown, otherwise hair just like a princess's in a fairy story (so Cora sometimes said, brushing it). Mr Inch also touched Emily's mother's hair in the same way: that was of course much shorter, which made it even curlier. But while Mr Inch touched Cora's hair in front of Emily, he never, Emily noticed, touched her own hair when Cora was present.

Emily paused to imagine what it would be like if Mr Inch got himself killed, like Emily's father. Would he explode like the old woman at the crossing? Sometimes Emily watched out of the window and saw Mr Inch approaching the house: he was supposed to cross by the zebra too (although sometimes he did not bother). Sometimes Emily would watch Mr Inch just running towards the house, galloping really, on his long legs. When Mr Inch visited Cora he always brought flowers, sweets for Emily, and sometimes a bottle of wine as well. After a bit Emily noticed that he began to bring food as well. He still managed to run towards their house, even carrying all these things.

When Mr Inch ran, he looked like a big dog. A big old dog. Or perhaps a wolf.

By now Emily had really grown out of fairy stories, including that story which her mother fondly imagined to be her steady favourite, Little Red Riding Boots. To tell the truth, she much preferred grown-up television; even if she did not understand it all, she found she understood more and more. Besides, Cora did not object.

That too, said Cora, was a form of protection.

'The news helps you to adjust painlessly . . . A child picks and chooses,' she told Mr Inch. 'Knowledge is safety . . . '

'But Cora, darling, there are some things you wouldn't want your sweet little Boots to know – I mean, what have you told her about us?'

Since this time neither Cora nor Mr Inch shut the door, Emily was left to reflect scornfully that there was no need for her mother to tell her about Mr Inch, since she saw him for herself, now almost every day, kissing her mother, touching her curly hair. And hadn't Mr Inch himself, while touching her hair, Emily's much longer hair, told Emily he hoped to come and live with them one day?

All the same, there was a resemblance between Mr Inch and a wolf. His big teeth. The way he smiled when alone with Emily, for example.

'All the better to eat you with – ' Emily could remember the story even if she could no longer be bothered to read it. Once, in spite of herself, she got out the old book and looked at her favourite picture – or rather, what had once been her favourite picture – of Grandmother in her frilly cap, Grandmother with big teeth, smiling.

Little Red Riding Boots stood in front of Grandmother, and though you could see the boots all right, all red and shiny, just like Emily's own, standing in the corner of her bedroom, you could not see the expression on the little girl's face. Nevertheless Emily could imagine that expression perfectly well. Definitely the little girl would not be looking afraid, in spite of everything, in spite of Grandmother's big teeth, in spite of being alone with her in the house.

This was because Emily herself was not afraid of Mr Inch, even when she was alone with him in the flat, and he called her his little girl, his little Boots (which Emily firmly ignored) and talked about all the treats he would give her 'one day', a day Mr Inch strongly hoped would come soon.

The girl in the picture was standing quite still. She knew that soon the woodcutter would come rushing in, as he did in the next picture, and save her. Then he would kill the wicked wolf, and in some books (not the version which was supposed to be her favourite) the woodcutter made a great cut in the wolf's stomach and out came, tumbling, all the other people the wolf had eaten. No blood, though, which was rather silly, because everyone knew that if you cut people open or knocked them or anything like that, there was masses of blood everywhere.

You saw it all the time in films when you were allowed to sit with your supper and hold your mother's hand during the frightening bits: 'Squeeze me, Boots, squeeze my hand.'

Emily loved sitting with Cora like this, to watch the films on television, and it was one of the things she really did not like about Mr Inch that when he arrived, Emily had to stop doing it.

Mr Inch watched the films with Cora instead and he held her hand; he probably squeezed it too. Sometimes he did other things. Once Emily had a bad dream and she came into the sitting-room. The television was still on but Mr Inch and Emily's mother were not watching it. Emily's mother lay on the floor all untidy and horrid, not pretty and tidy like she generally was, and Mr Inch was bending over her. His trousers were lying on the floor between Emily and the television, and Emily saw his long white hairy legs, and his white shirt tails flapping when he hastily got up from the floor.

Now that *was* frightening, not like a film or the news, and Emily did not really like to think about the incident afterwards. Instead she began to imagine, in greater detail how Mr Inch might get himself killed, like the wolf, like her father. She did not hold out much hope of Mr Inch going somewhere hot, because he never seemed to go anywhere, and also Mr Inch had plenty of money; lack of money was the reason that Emily's father had gone somewhere hot in the first place. Nor was he likely to be killed crossing the road, like the old woman, if only because Mr Inch was always warning Cora (and Emily) to take care; even when Emily watched Mr Inch running in their direction, she noticed that he always stopped for the lorries, and allowed plenty of time for them to pass. As for the woodcutter – which was a silly idea, anyway, because where would you find a woodcutter in a city? – even if you took it seriously, you would not expect a woodcutter to rush into their flat, because Cora saw so few people.

She was far too busy caring for her little girl, Cora explained to Mr Inch when they first met. Baby-sitters were expensive, and in any case unreliable.

'I shouldn't dream of trying to take you away from this dear little person,' Mr Inch had remarked on this occasion, flashing his big white teeth at Emily. 'It was always one of my great regrets that I never had a daughter of my own.'

No, Emily did not see how a woodcutter could be brought into the story. She wished that Mr Inch would be famous, and then he would go on television and maybe be killed. But Cora said that Mr Inch was not famous: 'Just a very good kind man, Boots, who wants to look after us.'

'Now I've got two little girls to look after,' said Mr Inch one day. For a moment Emily was mystified by his remark: she had a sudden hope that Mr Inch had found another little girl to look after somewhere else. It was only when Mr Inch took first Cora's hand, then Emily's, that she realized with a certain indignation that Mr Inch's other little girl was supposed to be her mother.

After that, the caring and looking-after by Mr Inch of Cora and Emily grew stronger all the time.

'I'll take very good care of her,' said Mr Inch, when Cora asked him to go down to the supermarket with Emily 'And I'm sure you won't object on the way back if there's just one ice-cream.'

'Run along, Boots,' called Cora from the kitchen, 'and hold Mr Inch's hand very tight. Specially crossing the road.'

Actually there was no need for Cora to mention crossing the road to Mr Inch, because he held Emily's hand so terribly tight on the way to the shops that she had to stop herself squeaking. Then Mr Inch cheated. He bought Emily not one but two ice-creams. He took her to the new Ice-Cream Parlour: Emily had never been inside before because Cora said it was too expensive.

Emily ate her ice-creams in silence. She was imagining cutting open Mr Inch with the woodcutter's axe: she did not think the things inside Mr Inch would be very nice to see (certainly no exciting people had been swallowed by Mr Inch). But there would be plenty of blood.

Even when Mr Inch asked Emily to come and sit on his lap and said that he had something very exciting to tell her, that he was going to be her new Daddy, Emily still did not say anything. She let Mr Inch touch her long hair, and after a bit she laid her head on Mr Inch's chest, which is what he seemed to want, but still she was very quiet.

'Poor little Boots is tired,' said Mr Inch. 'We'd better go home to Mummy.'

So Emily and Mr Inch walked along the crowded street, the short way back to their flat from the shops. Emily did not say anything and she did not listen to what Mr Inch was saying either. When Emily and Mr Inch got to the crossing, they paused and Emily – as well as Mr Inch – looked left, right and left again, just as Cora had taught her. This time Mr Inch was not holding Emily's hand nearly so tight, so it was Emily who squeezed Mr Inch's hand, his big hairy hand, and Emily who smiled at Mr Inch, with her little white pearly teeth.

It was when one of the really big lorries was approaching, the sort that Cora said shouldn't be allowed down their street, the sort which were rumbling their flat to bits, that the little red boots, shiny red plastic boots, suddenly went twinkling and skipping and flashing out into the road.

Fast, fast, went the little red boots, shining. Quick, quick, went the wicked wolf after the little red boots.

Afterwards somebody said that the child had actually cried out: 'Catch me! Catch me! I bet you can't catch me!' But Cora, even in her distress, said that couldn't possibly be true because Emily would never be so careless and silly on a zebra crossing. Hadn't Emily crossed it every day, sometimes twice a day, all her life? In spite of what the lorry driver said about the little girl dashing out and the man running after her, Cora still blamed the driver for the accident.

As for poor Mr Inch – well, he had died trying to save Emily, save her from the dreadful heavy lorry, hadn't he? He was a hero. Even if he was now a sad sodden lump of a hero, like an old dog which had been run over on the road.

Emily said nothing. Now Boots expected to live happily ever after with her mother, watching television, as in a fairy story.

Who Would Kill A Cat?

'Who on earth would want to do a thing like that?'

When the sodden dark-grey body of Wotan the cat was first discovered in the river at Chessworth, it was supposed that he had drowned. The whole group was there when he was fished out by Jacob Johnson: Felicity and her lover Jacob, who had been picnicking on the bank: Felicity's son Dickon, her daughter Poppet, and Felicity's brother, Deverill Cole, on his way back to the Manor after a longish walk. As Jacob was in the process of fishing out poor dead bedraggled Wotan from the weeds and branches encumbering the bank, the last member of the household – Letta, the *au pair* – turned up too, saying in her careful English that she had been looking for Poppet, 'in every place'.

Wotan, streaming water, looked more like a toy animal that had been accidentally immersed in a child's bath, than the feline prince he had been in life. Jacob, swallowing visibly, deposited his corpse on the bank, 'Poor Catto, poor old Catto.' Then with some feeling for order, he shifted the remains of the picnic things off the tartan rug, and deposited Wotan there in the centre of it. Wotan, lying amid scarlet checks, looked more like a toy than ever.

Felicity Maskell's eyes were full of tears, which although she made no sound, began to spill rapidly down her cheeks. Wotan had after all been her own darling pampered cat, her cat long before Chessworth Manor had been her home; the sight of Wotan lying there helpless and inanimate, brought back memories of Wotan the smokey kitten tumbling about her flat in Chelsea, Wotan delicately inspecting his new territory when she moved to Chessworth, Wotan the cat's jealousy of Poppet the new-born baby . . . Felicity suddenly realized that Poppet was standing beside her on the tufted green bank, a wilting posy of yellow wild flowers in her hand.

'Letta, please take Poppet back to the house at once,' Felicity spoke urgently.

At this point Poppet gave a loud cry of 'Furry! Oh poor Furry!' and started to cry very loudly, with her mouth open and her eyes screwed up, rather as she had cried when she was a baby, and Wotan a magnificent cat. Poppet added: 'He must have gone fishing and fallen in.'

By now Letta too was sobbing. No one could make out exactly what she was saying: '*Gatto*' and '*Morto*' being the only distinguishable words; Letta, never able to get her tongue round the word Wotan, had always referred to the cat as Gatto (it was from this that Jacob, when he first arrived at Chessworth, had derived 'Catto', saying that the name Wotan reminded him unpleasantly of Wagner).

'I'll take them both home,' Deverill Cole volunteered after rather a long pause. By this time Jacob had his arm round Felicity.

'Poor Puss, poor old Puss,' he was saying. 'There, darling, but it would have happened very quickly you know. Don't cry, darling.'

'What about that, then?' Dickon's uncertain voice of a sixteen-year-old sounded high and harsh at the same time. He stepped forward and gingerly touched a point near the dead cat's neck. It was then that the adult members of the party realized that something, hitherto invisible in the wet fur, was serrating Wotan's neck very tightly indeed.

In short, Wotan had been strangled before being thrown in the river. The current in the centre of the stream was so fast that it was surprising he had landed so quickly at the bank, still within the Chessworth domain, so to speak. But the green plastic-coated wire which killed him had caught on a submerged log, and so Wotan had come to rest only a few hundred yards from the home where he had lived the last eight years of his longish life.

'Who on earth would want to do a thing like that?' It was Dev who first used the words, but in the hours – and days – which followed, all of them asked the question in one form or another.

'Who would kill a *cat*?' cried Felicity. Her grief was both the most public and the most respected; her adoration of Wotan was after all not in question. Wotan the Wanderer had been given his Wagnerian name in the days when Felicity, a divorced woman living alone in Chelsea save for her small son Dickon, had been an ardent opera-goer. At that time it was Felicity who had been the wanderer, not the small fluffy grey cat, confined to a London flat. Yet the name had, to Felicity's mind, been strangely prescient; for when she married Edmund Maskell and transferred her tiny household consisting chiefly of Dickon and Wotan, to Chessworth, then the cat at last had lived up to his original appellation.

For many years now Wotan had wandered far and freely round the grounds and shrubberies of Chessworth, and even into the park, where he was believed to terrorize the small rodent population. It was because of these hunting expeditions that Wotan had not been missed on the day of his death. And although everyone agreed it made no difference in the long run, the fact that no one had been out searching for Wotan, that he lay for hours forgotten and lifeless, under the river bank, was nevertheless curiously upsetting.

It was good to remember that Edmund Maskell, Poppet's father, before his early death by cancer, had welcomed Wotan to Chessworth; 'Woe! Woe! he nicknamed him; a joke based on Wotan's destructive attitude to the brocade library curtains; which meant that the fine old material (which no one could afford to replace) soon hung in tatters. All the same, Edmund had been fond of Wotan, and so too – leaving aside his Wagnerian connections – was Jacob.

Jacob, a sculptor, had moved into Chessworth with Felicity and the children of her two marriages a year earlier. They did not plan to marry. Felicity, having been divorced and then widowed, was privately superstitious about subjecting the pleasantest relationship in her life to the possible bane of the wedding ring. After two neurotic husbands, to say nothing of a neurotic brother (Felicity did not even want to dwell on Dickon), what heaven to find Jacob! Anyway Jacob's own marital status was not clear: was he or was he not divorced from his wife, an artist currently living in America? Jacob himself did not know since the Johnsons had simply separated without discussion several years back, Jacob's work taking him to England, Alda Johnson's keeping her in the States. Felicity thought this meant that they were not divorced but Jacob was by no means certain.

'Wouldn't she have asked you for money or something, through her lawyers?'

'Money!' Jacob gave his jolly barking laugh. 'Even after all this time Alda knows me better than that; I might ask *her* for some money. Peter Stakovsky told me the other day her work is selling like hot cakes over there!'

It was true that Jacob's sculptures, huge, brightly coloured, like giant's meccano occupying the outbuildings at Chessworth, were not at present selling particularly well. He had made money in New York in the sixties, and expected confidently – he was a confident man, one of the many things which made him so agreeable to live with – to make money soon again: luckily his London dealer also predicted a renaissance of his popularity in the not-too-distant future. In the meantime Jacob lived at Chessworth, working hard in his white-washed outhouse studio, and with his naturally sweet disposition (it had to be said that poor Edmund, in the last painful stages of his illness had become fearfully bad tempered) made Felicity very happy.

If only Dev who was also, to put it bluntly, broke, and had

recently come to live with his sister at Chessworth, radiated something of Jacob's general enjoyment of life! Jacob managed to be so tender to all those around him, whatever his own problems – he was not only sweet to Poppet, which was easy, but also to Dickon, currently going through a very sulky phase. Dev was never conspicuously tender to anyone, with the possible exception of Letta, and although he was never conspicuously nasty either, his depression – a combination of ill-health (he was an asthmatic) and failure (he had been made redundant by his firm) – did make him a rather lowering companion.

'I wish I could help you, Flick, I'd like to do something for you,' Dev would say from time to time; his handsome face so like his sister's, taut with anxiety; but it was very difficult, for Felicity as well as Dev, to know exactly what this help could be. Felicity had after all one outstanding problem, and Dev could hardly assist with that: the problem of keeping Chessworth going for the sake of all these dependants she had somehow gathered round her.

Edmund's premature death, not long after the death of his own father, had left the Chessworth estate floundering. Most of the agricultural land had already been sold out of necessity, to pay the duties. What was left, really not much larger than Wotan's kingdom of park, garden, woods and shrubberies, might seem extensive for a cat; but it meant that Chessworth Manor itself, landless and needing extensive repairs, was not at present the kind of investment which might attract a wealthy buyer.

'So that it would probably be wrong to sell the Manor at this point. Wrong as well as heart-breaking. Until we've got things going.' Felicity concluded. 'Mending the roof for example.'

'Quite wrong,' exclaimed Jacob robustly. 'We'll hang on somehow. You'll see. I'll give Peter a ring; there's some kind of competition for a fountain at a new university.'

Dev, sitting broodily, with only the faint wheezing of his

breathing to denote his presence, rolled his eyes upwards. It was clear that he found Jacob's optimism intolerable.

'Who on earth would want to do a thing like that?' Dev enquired of the death of Wotan. The fact was that Dev, alone of the Chessworth household, had been hostile towards the cat. Admittedly his asthma, aggravated by Wotan's presence, gave him some excuse; but Felicity had always suspected that the true reason was jealousy. Dev, as Felicity's vulnerable younger brother, had always occupied a particular place in her affections; then Wotan had come as another vulnerable creature into her orbit. When Dev arrived at Chessworth, Felicity had to explain that it was impossible to bar Wotan from the library – in spite of Dev's asthma – because Wotan was used to leaping in and out of the big windows, and in summer they could hardly keep them closed. Dev received the news in silence, but his eyes looked somehow accusing; Wotan's eyes on the other hand, whenever he deigned to visit the library, looked magnificent, yellow and triumphant.

It was odd that Wotan, not Felicity's children, had aroused these emotions in Dev. But then Felicity was used to people – including Dickon and Poppet – exclaiming only half in fun: 'I think you love that cat better than anything in the world.'

Mind you, Dickon had his criticisms of Wotan too. At the age of six, he had suddenly announced that Wotan was hard-hearted and selfish.

'Mummy, you just don't see how hard-hearted he is.'

In adolescence Dickon had ritualized these criticisms into references to Wotan's callousness in killing young birds and bringing them into the house: Dickon seemed to think that Wotan, like himself, should aim at being vegetarian. But Dickon was the only person other than Felicity herself who called the cat by his proper name.

Poppet always referred to him as Furry, the name she had bestowed on him as a baby. From the first moment she had been able to stroke his wriggling form (held down by Felicity so that Wotan should be forced to overcome his jealousy of the baby) Poppet had loved Wotan so violently that Felicity had sometimes had to restrain her fierce hugs and kisses. But then Poppet, unlike Dickon, did everything violently, publicly.

'Who could do it? Who could do it?' she kept wailing aloud as she wandered round the house in the days following the discovery of Wotan's drowned body; and she gave up going down to the river altogether.

And the question did remain: who had done it? Someone had done it. Someone had pulled a piece of green plastic wire tightly round the animal's neck, and thrown the dead body into the river somewhere in the woods upstream, from which point, if luck had gone the killer's way, Wotan's corpse would have been carried rapidly away to join the main tributary of the river below.

'At least we *know*,' said Felicity brokenly at one point. 'I couldn't have borne not to know he was dead, just to wonder and search and call . . . that would have been ghastly. Days passing . . . Never to be sure.'

Jacob hugged her in his strong arms; like everyone else who loved Felicity at Chessworth, he had been wondering privately whether it would be tactless or therapeutic to introduce another cat into the household at this point. The rumour of a litter of kittens at an outlying farm was carried home by Dev, who alone of the family continued to take his long walks in the days following the tragedy; Dev mentioned this information in the kitchen when Felicity was out of the room. In his own way he seemed to be trying to atone for his known dislike of the late Wotan.

'Another Catto?' queried Jacob.

'No!' Dickon spoke sharply; this time his voice was husky. 'Mum couldn't stand it. And his name was Wotan.'

'In time,' said Jacob gently. 'Everything gets better with time.'

In the end, because Wotan's death was clearly the work of some vicious outsider – it was unthinkable that even asthmatic Dev would have risked causing Felicity such grief – the grown-ups fell back on murmuring about village vandals and insensitive louts, and blaming these traditional anonymous forces for the death of Wotan. The green plastic wire, for example was available in the Chessworth store, sold for gardening. Anyone, anyone at all, might have had a length of it handy in his pocket.

All the same it was odd – odd as well as horrible. The village of Chessworth was a good way away from the Manor; there was no school, and because there was no school, very few children of school age. Chessworth was a strangely quiet area at the best of times: if this was an act of vandalism, then it was the first such outrage to be encountered since Felicity had come to the Manor. Tramps passing through, poachers? It remained a disquieting as well as a distressing mystery.

Perhaps Felicity's family was additionally unsettled because July had already seen one major disturbance in the normally tranquil pattern of Chessworth life. A few weeks back there had been a burglary at the Manor: Felicity's jewellery had been taken – quite valuable things given to her by Edmund Maskell when they first married, belonging to his mother, as well as what remained of the Maskell family silver. In this case it was the feeling of unknown outsiders having penetrated their citadel which upset the household, rather than the event itself.

Once the shock was over of finding the downstairs lavatory window broken and the silver and jewellery gone – in the middle of the night, presumably, while they were all sleeping – Felicity got quite jolly on the subject.

'Thank God I kept up the insurance payments,' she kept repeating until Dev morosely asked her to stop. 'This could save our bacon. Those candlesticks, for example, I think they were index-linked, I think that's what Edmund arranged.'

Like the sense of unknown intruders, the frequent visits of the police (who drank a great deal of whisky) and a representative of the insurance company (who refused even sherry) were not particularly pleasant. However, in spite of diligent searchings of the Chessworth property, no substantial clues had yet been discovered, although the police told them enquiries were continuing. For the time being at least the insurance company, while promising further visits, seemed to be concentrating on the future security at the Manor – which Felicity for one found ridiculous: 'after all there's nothing left to steal'.

It was Poppet who first connected the two events: the robbery and the cat's death. 'Maybe Furry knew who the thief was and had to be silenced,' she began, rather fancifully. Then she suggested, even more fancifully, that one of the detectives had strangled the cat, out of spite, because he could not solve the case.

Felicity who was by now upset by any public mention of Wotan, told her quite sharply to be quiet.

Dickon however looked thoughtful.

To everyone's surprise, he had insisted on burying Wotan himself, using a black plastic sack as a coffin, and laying him gently in a secluded spot in the woods. Dickon explained that since he had known Wotan longer than anyone else – as long as his mother in point of fact, since he had gone with her as a little boy to collect the kitten – to bury him was his prerogative. Poppet was not allowed by Felicity to attend the ceremony; but Letta did so. Dickon said afterwards that she had muttered some incomprehensible prayers over the grave and cried a great deal: however, Felicity got the impression he was pleased at her attendance. Letta, although far too short for beauty, was not totally unattractive; certainly the T-shirt and jeans she habitually wore left little of her plump soft body to the imagination.

It would do Dickon good to talk more to Letta, who was not so many years older than he was and for that matter it would do Letta good not to talk quite so much to Dev; the latter must really be bored with Letta's languishing glances by this time, Felicity decided.

Yet the burial ceremony did not have an altogether good effect on Dickon's spirits. Poppet, who took to saying her own prayers for Furry at the little mound now that she was permitted to visit it, and leaving wild flowers there, reported one day rather hysterically that the grave had been disturbed.

Dickon bleakly claimed responsibility. All he would say

was that the grave had not been quite right before, and now it was. Possibly Letta knew something of the matter, but if so, she did not reveal it. Then Dickon took to going on very long walks in the woods and shrubberies, sometimes accompanied by Letta, more often than not. Letta once again was un-communicative on the subject when taxed by Felicity; and Felicity, in her mood of encouraging the friendship, did not like to press her.

Dickon's attitude at meals grew increasingly sombre. He hardly spoke at all. Jacob always saw it as his duty to be genial on these occasions: but now he failed to draw out Dickon. Even the melancholy Dev now seemed quite chatty in contrast to the boy.

'Where have you been today? Where did you go this afternoon?' Such questions received no reply at all or the curt: 'Nowhere in particular.'

'Should I do more about him? The man's role and all that?' Jacob questioned Felicity anxiously in private. Oddly enough, Dev, as Dickon's uncle, had recently addressed exactly the same question to Felicity. She advised them both to have patience. Dickon's father had been exceptionally moody. Besides Dickon was at the moody age. The mood – or the age – would change.

Then Dickon started going out at night.

This time Felicity really did protest. The burglary *and* the death of Wotan pointed to the fact that various unpleasant strangers were or had been around in the vicinity; she hardly thought it would be a good plan for Dickon to encounter one of them in the woods.

'I shan't,' Dickon said shortly.

'Oh Dickon, how can you be so certain? You're only sixteen – '

'I shan't encounter any strangers in the woods. You see I think I know why Wotan was killed. And tomorrow I'm going to prove it to you.'

Conscious that as a parent she was ever torn between worry and permissiveness, Felicity compromised by consulting

Jacob. Jacob, as a surrogate parent ever more permissive than worried, thought Dickon should be allowed to work out what was biting him. Dev, whom Felicity also consulted, said rather sardonically that he saw no harm in Dickon at the age of sixteen laying Letta in the woods – if that's what he really wanted to do; but maybe Dev minded Letta's defection to Dickon more than she had supposed.

'See you in the morning then,' Felicity ended to Dickon.

But Felicity never did see Dickon again. Or rather, when she next saw her son he was dead, reduced by death – and the blow of a spade to the head – to someone with only a mysterious resemblance to the child she had once had. For Dickon was found lying where he had fallen in the woods; his head tipped back where he had been hit with his own spade; and where in falling, he had been pierced by the cruel sharp spike of a broken tree.

The death itself was probably an accident, said the police. But the Detective Chief Inspector commented privately to his subordinate: 'Whoever it was may not have meant to kill him, but he certainly hit him bloody hard with that spade.'

Dickon's body half covered a deep hole, deep in the soft earth, dug through a great layer of long rotted leaves, wet even in summer. Felicity's jewellery and the Chessworth Manor silver lay within it, partially exposed from a sack. Soft rich earth had fallen on the blackened silver of the candlesticks. The police said that Dickon would have died more or less instantly. There were signs that his killer had made some efforts to establish that fact – had even tried to revive him – before, leaving the silver and jewellery, he had fled.

'The Gatto, it was the Gatto,' wept Letta hysterically. 'It was the Gatto who has found the treasure. He has told me.'

'Now, my dear,' said the detective in a very kindly voice, for he had daughters of his own and one of them had even worked in Italy, so that he felt he had sympathetic knowledge of the country, 'Tell me all about it in your own words.'

Unfortunately for all her sobs, and even after an Italian interpreter was called in, Letta never seemed to get much further than the fact that Dickon had told her the cat had been killed for digging up what she called the 'tesorio' – the treasure. And Dickon knew who had done it. He had found the earth under the cat's claws when he buried him, and checked again on the cat's corpse for the right kind of soil, and had – as it appeared – finally found the right place. But he had not told Letta who was the killer – that is, the killer of the Gatto.

The detectives examined every member of the stricken household – including, in a gentle way and in the presence of Felicity, Poppet. Statements were taken.

Not only Letta gave a statement, but Felicity and Dev and Jacob. Dev was there for a long time. Jacob followed him. Felicity sat with Dev, waiting for Jacob to emerge. She did not ask Dev what he had said. Dev did not tell her.

Who would kill a cat? Perhaps a person who had hidden valuables from the police's constant searchings would suddenly kill a cat, when that cat constantly followed him, scratched up the hoard under the leaves, wandering, scratching, never leaving the hiding place alone. A quick tug of wire: after all what was a cat's life?

Who would strike down Dickon? Perhaps the same person, who had already taken the law into his own hands and faked the robbery at Chessworth Manor for the sake of the insurance money to help Felicity. He might have taken the law into his hands again, suddenly seeing no difference in going still further and striking down his accuser.

One thing was sure: the police, who would not have cared to investigate the death of Wotan the cat, would in their remorseless way, sooner or later discover the murderer of Dickon.

Now the real torture came to Felicity. And in her torture she looked towards Dev, found herself looking at Dev with tragic wide open eyes, looking at him perhaps properly for the very first time.

Dev. Her brother. Her brother who had always wanted to

help her: 'I wish I could do something, Flick.' He could do something now.

Dev would have to be her prop, the only one left to her. Dev would now have to be the strong one. Together they would sell Chessworth and together they would live in London.

Even if Jacob did not confess to the police, Felicity was going to denounce him: Jacob who had gaily organized the robbery, with her connivance, to get them both out of financial difficulties; but in doing so had found it necessary to kill her cat, carelessly, secretly, not confiding in her, not thinking it really mattered at all. Jacob who always looked to the future – there would be another cat – and Jacob who, with equal confidence, had promised her that no harm would ever come to her or her family while he was in charge.

Who would kill a cat? The same careless confident man who would in the end kill, however unintentionally, her child.

Doctor Zeit

'I'm being pursued by this face,' she thought. 'This old face. I'm frightened. I'll have to do something.'

The first time Nola saw the face she was in the Underground, on the moving stairs coming up to the Tottenham Court Road. The last leg of the journey. Nola always felt like a seal coming up for air at Tottenham Court Road tube with its double staircase. She began to breathe deeply as she reached the top. Nola was not particularly strong and she felt she needed all the air she could get before she reached the British Museum, and the somewhat airless atmosphere of its Reading Room.

Nola had been working for the past two years on a study of seventeenth-century family life. She still had a long way to go. From time to time she told her publisher, lightly, that twentieth-century family life came first. Which meant the house in Islington with the lovely wooden polished floors, kitchen often full of healthy foods, large country-style garden – all of them rivals for her attention with the British Museum.

And, of course, there were Denis and Johnnie. Denis was Nola's husband and Johnnie was her son. To Nola, privately, they were the perfect family unit. She had no wish for another child. Denis protected Nola – he was much older than her – and Nola protected Johnnie. Indeed, when she thought about Johnnie's small but perfectly made body, Nola imagined that she felt the same joy that Denis often told her he felt in her youth, her beauty (because of the difference in their age, he said, to him she would always look young, no matter how the years passed).

On her route to and from the British Museum, Nola's favourite thoughts were of the two of them. She was meditating on Johnnie and how perfect he was, and how in a way she wished he could stay five years old forever, so gay, so ebullient, so amusing, so much her little boy . . . when she felt a slight tug on her long skirt. Nola turned round. The staircase was not particularly crowded – it was after ten o'clock and the workers had vanished to their offices. Several steps below her a woman with a very old face was smiling at her. At least Nola thought at the time that she was a woman, but she was so very old, judging from her face at least, that she had already reached that stage of asexuality of appearance which makes it difficult to tell the inhabitants of male and female geriatic wards apart.

Nola had certainly never seen the woman before in her life. Nola presumed therefore that she had dropped something. But her bag was standing neatly intact on the step above her. She checked it, looked round again, missed the old woman completely, found the top of the staircase claiming her attention, searched for her ticket and forgot the incident.

The second time that Nola saw the face, it was definitely on a man. On him – that was how she instinctively put it to herself because despite the fact that the face was exactly the same as the previous face, old, really old, seamily wrinkled flesh hanging round the jowls, wispy hair, she got the odd impression that she was not seeing the same person so much as the same face.

On this occasion she saw the face and its bearer standing on the platform of Tottenham Court Road tube station as her train drew in. She had a quick uncomfortable flash of recognition and the face – the man rather – seemed to feel likewise because he gave a little salute with his hand. The other hand held a stick. When Nola got off the train, he was gone.

He had presumably entered the train elsewhere where it was less crowded.

The third occasion she saw the face was more disturbing. It was Johnnie's half-term. Nola had a choice of staying at home with him or taking him along with her, since Denis was of course at the office. She decided to take him on a visit to the British Museum: not into the Reading Room, of course; that was out of the question, perish the thought of introducing rumbustious Johnnie into such a sanctum even if it had been permitted. But she did think it would be rather pleasant to show Johnnie some of the sights, the Elgin Marbles, vast sphinxes, statues, the sort of thing that an intelligent five-year-old would find quite stimulating to the imagination without precisely understanding them. And she would point to the door of the Reading Room, perhaps, and call it 'Mum's office'. Johnnie knew about offices. He had visited Denis's office on several occasions. When Denis returned in the evening, Johnnie used to chant: 'Backfromtheoffice' as if it was all one word. They set off early so as to be back for Johnnie's lunch.

But Johnnie and Nola never got as far as the British Museum. At Tottenham Court Road station ('This is where Mum comes to work in the morning'), the most awful thing happened. Johnnie disappeared. One moment he was holding Nola's hand, the next moment there was a sharp tug and he was gone. Through the pressing crowd, he vanished completely. Nola was distraught, sick with fear.

'Johnnie, Johnnie!' she screamed, turning round and trying to battle her way against the incoming crowd.

She struggled back finally on to the platform from whence they had come. And saw two things. Johnnie, tearful, holding the hand of a black Underground inspector, who was bending down and trying to comfort him. For a split second she also saw that face, that old face. She would know it anywhere. But this time on quite a young and sturdy body: she had the impression of jeans, a T-shirt. The man, woman, whatever it was, smiled and vanished down the far exit to the other line.

Johnnie, sobbing, seemed to expect Nola to punish him. In self-defence he talked of a horrible old man with a nasty smell pulling him away.

'I couldn't help it. He was much stronger than me,' he kept saying.

'Darling, we're going straight home,' was all Nola could bring herself to reply.

When she told Denis about it in the evening – an edited version not mentioning the previous encounters with the face – he said quite sharply:

'Wasn't it rather silly to take a kid to the BM in the first place? I mean, you can go there as much as you like when he's at school. I shouldn't think it would have been quite his cup of tea if you had got there. He's still at the playground stage if you ask me.'

Nola, feeling guilty, forbore to mention her plan of showing Johnnie the door of 'Mum's office'. Denis was right. Johnnie had not yet reached the sightseeing stage: she was the one who did not want him to grow up too fast, and now she was trying to force the pace.

The fourth, fifth and sixth times Nola saw the face were in and around Islington when she was shopping or on her way to fetch Johnnie from school. On each occasion the face smiled at her. Johnnie was right: it was definitely an old man. The impression of a youthful body and jeans that day must have been part of her general distraction at losing the child. The truth was, she told herself, that he was just a rather mad old man who happened to live in Islington and filled in the time leering at young women . . . Perfectly harmless if unpleasant. Nola pulled herself up: not *totally* harmless, if her theory was correct. The old man had tried to kidnap Johnnie. No, that was really going much too far in the other direction. Kidnap was far too strong a word. Denis had been quite right when he pointed out that Johnnie was only a child, had been known to wriggle his hand free under other circumstances.

'Probably just didn't want to go to the BM,' said Denis with a smile. He worried a little all the same – not about Johnnie but about Nola. Nola, of all the women he knew, was the most conscientious mother. And wife. And then there was her book. And her health. Health, which was never strong and could too easily lead to nervousness and collapse if Nola overstretched herself. However, Denis and Nola had agreed long ago when they first married never to refer to Nola's condition and to live their lives exactly as if it did not exist. So that Denis decided to say nothing more on this occasion, only to watch Nola more carefully in future. At least he could try and see that she did not overdo the British Museum stuff.

But, of course, Nola's projected book had to have its place in her life, along with the house and the garden and the creative kitchen and Denis and Johnnie. The idea had originated as a post-graduate thesis suggested by Nola's tutor, who had a high opinion of her work. It was a task to which marriage to Denis and the birth of Johnnie put an end. Only temporarily, however. Nola got back to it once Johnnie went to nursery school. And it was really much more fun doing it in terms of a proper book, being her own mistress as it were, without the inevitable restraints of the structure of a thesis. Besides which she no longer needed a grant to support herself while working on it.

'You're my grant,' she told Denis. 'And a very nice grant too.'

If Nola's progress was slow – school holidays were an interruption – at least it was steady. And she never found any difficulty in picking up her work again where she had left off: the mere entry into the atmosphere of the Reading Room, airless as it might be, transported her. It was in its own way like a Secret Garden to which Nola – and admittedly five hundred others – had the key.

So that it was fantastically upsetting one morning, as she arrived later than her schedule, to see the face, sitting three along from the seat she usually occupied. Not in her seat, thank God, that would have been too much; might have persuaded her she was seeing an apparition, a sort of *doppelgänger*, an aged version of herself – but she wasn't seeing an apparition, she knew that. This old woman – and she was definitely a woman this time – was real. What was more, as Nola flung down her bag on her seat, the woman with the old face got up and shuffled off in the direction of the North Library. The old face did not smile, Nola noticed, there was a nasty set grumpy look about the mouth above the hanging dewlaps. On the whole, Nola preferred this air of crossness, even anger, to the original leer. Besides which the old woman had left her books behind on the table. Nola could see them lying there.

Now was her chance to find out a little more about her pursuer. With a feeling of determination, Nola strode down the row of desks and picked up the book lying open. She nearly dropped it with surprise. It was Levin Schücking's *Puritan Family*. It was a comparatively new book which had come out since Nola began working on her subject and Nola had made quite a bit of use of it herself. She did not know why she was so surprised at the sight of it on the old woman's desk. It was a most disagreeable sensation.

Still more disagreeable was the discovery that the other four books on the desk were all pertaining to the subject of women and marriage in the seventeenth century – or as you might put it, seventeenth-century family life. Some of them were quite obscure.

Nola took a decision. She put in a slip for Schücking's book, and duly got her slip returned with the scribbled information on the back that it was 'Out to another reader': she could not quite read it but the name looked like Zett. Nola went to the centre desk and explained her problem.

'The old lady who has it out is sitting quite close to me as a matter of fact. But she went out an hour ago and hasn't returned. So I wondered if I could just check something . . .'

'Name?' said the man behind the desk with professional politeness but without interest.

'Zett, it looks like, or Zelt.'

The man's face clouded.

'Oh, dear. Old Mrs Zeit. Or rather Frau Doktor Zeit as she

prefers to be called. Oh, dear. Well, I'll see what I can do when she comes back.'

'Is she – er?' Nola pursued delicately, prompting, not finishing the sentence. The man grinned and raised his eyebrows. She saw that he was quite young.

'Shall we say that she's a little difficult?' he said. 'We get them in here. Delusions of persecution. Probably a refugee from somewhere. She thinks everyone is trying to steal her researches from her before she can write her book – '

'And her book is on – ?'

The young man took thought.

'Seventeenth-century family life,' he answered. 'Something like that.'

He was surprised when Nola, who had seemed such a pleasant person, turned on her heel abruptly and marched out of the Reading Room. Actually Nola was going to the Ladies' because she felt dizzy. And when she came back she just collected her bag and left. Frau Doktor Zeit was not there. All the same, she knew she could not do any work that day.

This was the point at which Nola thought: 'I'm being pursued by this face. This old face. I'm frightened. I shall have to do something.'

She told Denis that she had discovered an old woman in the Reading Room who was working on exactly the same subject as herself – and for a book, too; she felt that it was a catastrophe. That was as far as Nola could bring herself to relate recent events for the time being. If Denis were sympathetic – and she knew he would be – she could probably nerve herself to discuss the face itself thereafter.

'Don't go to the British Museum, darling, for a bit,' said Denis immediately. 'You've had a shock. I can see that. Not that some old crone is really going to write a book and steal your thunder. Not a chance. Your book will be terrific when it comes out, never fear. But the truth is you've been overdoing it lately. A rest – here at home – will freshen you up. Work twice as hard when you get back to it.'

'I've got so much to get through,' Nola began rather desperately. Denis soothed her. 'Darling, I know.'

'But the time's passing – '

'There's plenty of time. For one thing Johnnie won't be a baby for ever. He won't need fetching and carrying from school forever.'

'And I suppose you're going to grow out of needing a hot dinner at night,' said Nola wryly.

'Exactly,' Denis beamed. 'My teeth will soon fall out. Then I shan't be able to eat anything but cereal. That means you won't have to cook at all.'

Nola looked worried again. 'Don't talk like that,' she begged. 'On top of everything else. You know I can't bear to think of you getting old.'

It was the solitary hang-up she had about the disparity in their ages. She could not bear a mention of such things, even a light reflection like the fact that Denis would be sixty-five and retiring when Johnnie was twenty-one and going out to work, caused her to shiver.

'Now Nola,' said Denis, taking her in his arms. 'You really are out to upset yourself, aren't you? As for me, I'm in the pink of health. I had the firm's annual medical check-up today. I forgot to tell you with all this going on. I'm AI OK the doctor told me. The physique of a young man. Not so the doctor himself, I must say. Talking of the old, this was the oldest fellow I have ever seen. I thought I must have made a mistake when I stepped into the consulting-room. He looked just like a tortoise.'

'A man with a very old face?' Nola asked carefully, after a pause.

'That's right. He might have been Methuselah himself. But he gave me a clean bill of health. Wait a moment, darling, I'm crazy. You *know* him. When I said goodbye, he asked me to give you his love. You and Johnnie. But especially you. He's an Austrian. Doctor Zeit I think his name was – why, darling!'

As Denis held Nola, he felt her go slack and heavy in his arms. She had fainted.

'It was nothing,' said Nola a minute later when she found herself sitting on the sofa. 'Just one of my turns. Don't fuss me. You promised.' She saw Denis's anxious face leaning over her and went on: 'Don't *worry* . . .' It was like when they were first married. Her one concern was to reassure him about her.

But Denis did worry. Despite Nola's protests, he insisted on putting her to bed for the rest of the evening. In return, he promised not to fuss her too much the next day.

Nevertheless, Nola did not even try to go to the British Museum. She did not feel up to it. And she kept Johnnie at home too although Denis did not know that till later. He generally left for the office before Johnnie went to school. All the same Nola was determined not to waste the day entirely. She pondered between the rival claims of kitchen and garden. A day cooking for the deep freeze? Or a day really tidying up the garden before the onset of winter? In the end the garden won, because Nola had to admit that the garden was showing signs of positive neglect whereas the kitchen wasn't. When Denis telephoned her later that morning, ostensibly to consult her about an invitation, Nola told him:

'By the way, I'm clearing up the garden. It's rather fun.'

'Just the ticket.' Denis managed to sound delighted. 'It's a beautiful day for it too. I walked half the way to the office.'

Nola dug a little, created a pile of rubbish and finally went indoors with the laudable intention of doing to the airing cupboard what she had just done for the garden. She was upstairs on a ladder, reaching for the back of the cupboard when she heard the front door-bell ring. Nola hesitated and looked at Johnnie.

'Johnnie, could you?'

"Course I could,' he said contemptuously. Later Johnnie shouted something up the stairs about the garden. Nola was rather puzzled. She ought really to go down – but Johnnie had panted back up the stairs again.

'Daddy sent someone to do the garden for you. So I let him through the back door,' he said importantly.

'Oh, I see.' Nola was taken aback and suddenly rather

chilled. Hadn't she been going to do the garden herself? Denis was treating her like a baby again, not wanting her to strain herself.

Presently Nola looked out of the window and saw the gardener's back. He was wearing jeans and to her surprise he appeared to be wielding a scythe. She looked again. Yes, it was definitely a scythe. In their garden and at this time of year! What was Denis thinking of?

Johnnie was in his room, playing with his little cars in the window-seat. Nola gave him a quick glance and then clattered down the stairs and into the garden.

'Excuse me,' she said in a voice of authority. 'What are you doing with that scythe?' The young man stood up and turned round. He was still holding his scythe as he moved towards Nola. His voice was quite young and musical when he replied: 'I'm caring for your garden. Don't worry. I shall be here to care for it after you are gone.'

But his face was an old face, a familiar face.

Johnnie, looking out of the window, saw his mother fall down and lie still. Later he described to his father exactly the man who had come to do the garden, the man with the scythe, in jeans, but a man with a terribly old face. He told his father that the man with the terribly old face had cut down his mother with his scythe. But that was nonsense, of course; a child's reaction to shock. There was not a mark on Nola's body.

On The Battlements

It was at least three o'clock in the morning and there was Letty coming out of the cottage next door. Melanie could see her quite clearly. The Italian night never seemed quite dark, or was it because all the stars were still out? In any case, there was no mistaking Letty: all that hair.

'Like a fox with a thick brush,' thought Melanie. And there was altogether something of a nocturnal animal about the way Letty paused and seemed to sniff the night air. She was poised gracefully on the doorstep; one paw was raised; then Letty padded across the grass back to the main house. The thought of the house brought Melanie round sharply to the subject of Letty's husband Victor. It was of course Alistair Drummond who was sleeping in the cottage. For a moment, sleepily, she had supposed it must be Victor. But she had put Letty and Victor upstairs in the two single rooms in their Tuscan farmhouse. Victor was an actor and said by Letty to be extremely exhausted after a taxing season at Stratford, hence the separate rooms. Alistair, as the odd man out, or the unhappy bachelor (as he preferred to term it) had been put in their cottage annexe. Not so unhappy tonight, it seemed, with a visit from Letty . . .

Letty and Alistair . . . and Victor asleep upstairs . . . Really, Letty was a *lunatic*. Melanie underlined the word fiercely in her own thoughts. Supposing Victor woke up? Surely even the most successful season could hardly be guaranteed to provide total immobility? And then Victor was so attractive, and the marriage was hardly more than a year old, even if Letty had had an affair with him for a long time before that. Victor with his handsome open face, Melanie searched it in her mind's eye, a sort of latter-day Leslie Howard. Was Letty bored with Victor already or was it the fact of marriage which did not suit her? Then *Alistair*, more underlinings in Melanie's mind, that irresponsible boy with his energy and his springy red hair. Perhaps Letty had a penchant for red hair? Were red-haired men more passionate . . . Victor had thick fair hair which Melanie personally much preferred, but she had to admit she was an innocent in these matters, depending, to tell the truth, a great deal on Letty for guidance in them. Well, there was no guidance to be had from Letty at this hour of the night. At least Ralph had not woken up, that was something to be thankful for; the dark shape in their bed did not stir. Baulked of she knew not quite what prey, Melanie slid carefully between the sheets beside him and fell into sleep.

Although it was still only May, the next morning the sun was so hot that no one had the energy to go sightseeing. In the original decision by Ralph to purchase a farm-house in Tuscany, the prospect of frequent cultural expeditions – to Siena, to Florence – had played much part. Melanie suspected that he enjoyed the organization of such outings as much if not more than the fulfilment of them. Now Ralph gazed at their guests, clustered under the olive trees planted round the swimming-pool, like cows seeking the shade. Letty was rubbing sun-oil into Victor's back with Alistair loudly demanding his turn. To Melanie's watchful gaze it was all innocent enough, if not very active.

'We'll wait till the evening,' announced Ralph 'and then climb up the battlements at Belcaro. You can see right over to Siena.'

'It's ravishing there in the twilight,' added Melanie. 'Most romantic.'

'I'm all for a spot of that,' said Alistair with enthusiasm. It was, Melanie had to admit, the sort of remark he would probably have made anyway. Letty continued to rub Victor's white back, with its ruffle of blond hairs along the spine, with delicate strokes of her fingers.

'Perhaps, Victor, you wouldn't mind reciting something for us?' continued Ralph. 'The battlements have these fantastic acoustics. I've always wanted to hear a really magnificent voice like yours make use of them. Even better than the stage at Stratford.' Ralph was referring to Victor's recent much-acclaimed performance of Henry V.

'A treat!' exclaimed Letty. She was in a very good mood this morning, the cat, thought Melanie, fox last night, cat this morning, the cat who had had its bowl of cream. There was definitely something feline about Letty when she was contented. But Victor too seemed content. Did he know anything? Melanie had scrutinized his face at breakfast with morbid care. It was as amiable as anyone could wish. It was of course possible that he was acting a part. After all Victor *was* an actor and presumably could act in private if he chose. On the other hand as he generally played such heroic parts on the stage – the complement to his equable nature in private – would he really be capable of dissimulating a tranquillity he did not feel? It was a conundrum and Melanie gave it up in favour of pouring coffee. She felt herself rewarded when throughout the day Victor remained placid, agreeable, good mannered. Intermittently he studied a new part. Alistair, in contrast, tended to bound restlessly about the pool area, chattering, laughing, teasing Letty, and, presumably, disturbing Victor.

'All the same, Mel, I'm glad you asked that Alistair,' Ralph observed at six o'clock, as he prepared himself for the evening's expedition by shaving. Melanie watched him as he stood in the rather primitive new bathroom created for their joint needs. Beyond Ralph's head a window framed a perfect view of hills, cypresses, and the reddish tower of an occasional villa, which might have formed the background for any of the pictures they admired so industriously in their sightseeing.

Ralph continued: 'Funny chap, Victor, he's awfully quiet in private, isn't he? I mean, I'm terribly fond of him, but he's not a bit like he is on stage, always waving swords and shouting. Awfully good manners and all that, but almost dull in a way.'

'Letty likes him. He suits her,' said Melanie. She hoped it was true.

'You would have thought that Letty would have gone for someone a little more fiery, though, a little more go in him.'

'I suppose she can always watch Victor on the stage for all that,' replied Melanie vaguely. 'I mean, actors have that advantage, don't they?'

Ralph scraped and grimaced and talked. 'All the same, I wouldn't mind if the old boy did a bit more bounding about the swimming-pool and waving a sword and shouting at lunch-time.' He paused appreciatively. 'Like Alistair. What is more, I bet old Letty wouldn't mind either.'

They took two cars to Belcaro. Letty sat in front of the big English estate car which Alistair drove, and Melanie – she had to admit the motive to herself – chaperoned them from the back. That left Victor and Ralph in the Fiat.

'I'll prepare Victor for his part,' said Ralph. 'Romeo perhaps. I'll never forget your Romeo, Victor. *It is the east and Juliet is the sun* . . . Give or take the time of day of course.' But whatever success Ralph was having in the Fiat with his directing, Melanie's chaperonage in the estate car was a complete failure. Letty unashamedly kissed Alistair's cheek while he was driving, and Alistair, even more boldly, put his left hand in Letty's lap. Finally Melanie could bear it no longer.

'Letty, does Victor know about all this?' she burst out, while Alistair was temporarily out of the car paying for petrol.

'Of course not. Victor hasn't the least idea.' Letty sounded quite shocked. The trouble was that Melanie could think of no effective way of remonstrating with her. There was something so reckless, no reckless was too weak a word, so, well, violent, about the way Letty threw herself at situations that the very violence carried you along with it. Ralph was right. In a way it was hardly surprising that Letty found herself bored with the mild and disarming Victor.

As the blue of the sky began to deepen, the castle of Belcaro rose up above their heads out of a dark sea of protecting foliage. It seemed to have no connection with the surrounding plain.

'A castle in a fairy-tale,' exclaimed Letty. 'Could that be a rose hedge?'

'Ilexes for Sleeping Beauty,' said Melanie.

'And you're the princess,' said Alistair with a quick fond smile sideways at Letty. 'If not always so sleepy,' he added. Yes it was fortunate the two parties were separated. However, when both cars, having passed the ilex barrier, drew up together outside the postern gates of the castle, its very scale, the immensity of the masonry, the oppressive quiet of the remote fortress, united them. It was as though they were all travellers seeking shelter.

'It's too late. It's shut,' said Letty suddenly. She looked tiny against the gate and slightly defiant. But it was surely out of the question that Letty would be pleased at the abandonment of an adventure.

'No, no,' said Ralph, 'I telephoned the caretaker. They'll let us in. We've done it before. Push the gate, Letty, and see.' Letty pushed the heavy iron-barred gate. This time Melanie had a distinct feeling that Letty, devil-may-care Letty, was in some way nervous. Alistair ran forward to help her. Together they headed the procession up the path inside the first wall, which led to another smaller door. Alistair opened it and Letty passed in. Then Victor walked past them both and stood gazing out at the prospect revealed in the interior. Unexpectedly the battlements on which they now stood looked down into a courtyard in which a complete house, perhaps of the Renaissance period, had been built against one wall of the castle. One or two lights already showed there. The battlements circled round it, punctuated from time to time by little flights of steps and miniature turrets. Ralph was right. The effect was extraordinarily theatrical.

'It positively calls for a performance,' exclaimed Ralph. 'Perfect for *Romeo and Juliet.*'

'Somehow I thought of *Macbeth*,' replied Victor. His back was still turned.

'You mean the crow is making wing to the rooky wood?' contributed Melanie hopefully. It was the line she knew best in the play. Victor did not answer.

'I think it's everything that *Romeo and Juliet* ought to be!' cried Letty. Ralph took Melanie's hand and squeezed it. Melanie guessed that Alistair might be doing the same thing to Letty, but in any case Victor, who was ahead, would hardly notice. The little party, under Victor's leadership, filed along the battlements towards the far turret. The lights of Siena twinkling in the distance made the town look like a gold crown spread out on the ground. The glow of the courtyard became more prominent and the sky began to lose its colour.

'Midnight blue,' said Letty in a poetic voice.

'It's about eight o'clock blue actually.' That was Alistair, making a joke as usual. 'I've got those eight o'clock blues.'

'Curtain up!' Ralph ignored Alistair's attempts at crooning. 'Now, Victor, give us your all.' Victor turned round, and backed a few steps up the turret so that he gazed down on his audience. He looked extraordinarily handsome in the waning light, a beseeching lover, a chivalrous knight from a Burne Jones picture. Victor raised his eyes beyond their heads, and when he began to speak in his beautiful voice, it was like the consummation of romance.

'*Tomorrow and tomorrow and tomorrow*,' began Victor, his voice echoing round the battlements as Ralph had promised it would, '*creeps on this petty pace from day to day, to the last syllable of recorded time . . .*' Melanie's reaction was of sheer surprise. She had been in such complete expectation of Shakespeare's tender love sonnets, that it was as if Victor had in some way jumped his lines. But when Victor pronounced the words ' '*tis a tale told by an idiot*', it was said with such savage fury, that Melanie turned instinctively to Letty, 'I had thought somehow a sonnet – '

157

'So did I.'

'It's so romantic up here.'

'Evidently Victor doesn't think so.'

'Letty, do you think perhaps that after all Victor? . . .'

'Out of the question. He just likes *Macbeth*. The place reminds him of it. He said so when we first arrived.'

'It reminds the rest of us of *Romeo and Juliet*.'

But Victor followed up his lines from *Macbeth* with a speech beginning: *Behold yon simpering dame* and containing, to Melanie, the hardly reassuring words.

'*Down from the waist they are centaurs*
Though women all above . . .'

Letty was frowning.

'It's King Lear, the mad scene,' she whispered to Melanie. 'I remember it because Victor played Edgar at the National. The speech begins with something about the adultery . . .' Now Victor was on ground more familiar to Melanie. '*Get thee to a nunnery, why wouldst though be a breeder of sinners? . . .* That was hardly the essence of romance. It was true that Victor had played Hamlet only one season back, but surely one of the famous soliloquies might be more appropriate? Ralph's voice echoed her thoughts:

'How about *To be or not to be*, then?' he said with undiminished heartiness. Had Ralph not noticed the gathering violence in Victor's tone? Victor responded, if it was a response, by delivering instead, '*Oh what a rogue and peasant slave am I*' in tones of such unsuppressed passion (surely he had not given the speech like that at Stratford) that the famous words seemed quite robbed of any element of traditional indecision, while the battlements fairly rang to '*Bloody, bawdy villain! Remorseless, treacherous, lecherous, kindless villain.*' And Victor chose to end the speech on the simple words '*O Vengeance!*' Melanie did not dare look at Letty.

'It's past eight o'clock,' she said. 'Should we be thinking of dinner?'

But Alistair too was uncontaminated by the atmosphere. 'One last poem from Victor!' he suggested.

'Victor hasn't given us a proper poem yet.' It was Ralph. He sounded childish and disappointed. Victor started to intone again.

'It is the cause, it is the cause, my soul,
Let me not name it to you, you chaste stars,
It is the cause – '

'Oh my God, it's Othello,' thought Melanie. For greater effect – or unbearable tension? – Victor now turned his back on them again and delivered his lines towards the darkness of the plain where Siena now looked a far-distant and unattainable haven.

'When I have plucked the rose,' hissed Victor in that low but carrying voice that only actors possess, *'I cannot give it vital growth again, it needs must wither.'* And then, equally low, equally frenetic: *'One more, and this the last: So sweet was ne'er so fatal. I must weep, but they are cruel tears: this sorrow's heavenly; It strikes where it doth love.'* As he finished speaking, Victor wheeled round. Melanie had time to realize that Letty and Alistair must have been holding hands in the darkness before they sprang apart. The whole episode reminded her of a sinister version of Grandmother's Footsteps.

'Now walk with me, Letty,' said Victor.

Letty laughed. 'It's too narrow to walk together, darling,' she said. Her voice sounded amused but Melanie was suddenly prompted to look down at her hands, white in the dusk. They were touching each other at the finger-tips, twisting each other, praying nervous hands. Beside them the battlement dropped sheer to the ground on one side and to the courtyard on the other.

'She really is frightened,' thought Melanie. Suddenly her own fear drove out everything else like a drum in her mind. Victor does know, Victor does know, Victor as Othello, Victor does know.

Victor turned back and walked forward. His voice – this time without invitation – was heard again: *'My wife! My wife! What wife? I have no wife. O insupportable! O heavy hour! Methinks it should be now a huge eclipse of sun and moon, and that*

the affrighted globe should yawn at alteration.' Dear God, would
he now leave Othello alone?

'Letty,' she said urgently, throwing caution away. 'He must
know.'

'He *can't*,' Letty still remembered to whisper, but it was a
fierce whisper. She added, contradicting herself: 'I'm terrified.
Victor's gone mad.'

*'Who can be wise, amaz'd, temperate and furious, loyal and
neutral in a moment? No man. The expedition of my violent love
outran the pauser reason . . .'* What was this? Oh, Macbeth
again, well at least that was getting away from Othello.

'Victor has never *played* Macbeth,' whispered Letty. 'I don't
understand it.'

'Well, he's certainly playing it now . . .'

'Macduff, yes, Banquo I think twice, but never Macbeth.'
Letty seemed obsessed by Victor's theatrical past.

'Well, has he played Othello?'

'Of course not; can you imagine Victor as Othello? The
audience would burst into roars of laughter. The perfect
English hero . . . no paint would be black enough to convince
them.'

'I think he's playing that now too.' And it was true. With
grandiloquent flourishes, Victor was zipping his way through
most of the words of Othello, pausing only for breaths which
were more sucked than swallowed. In its own way it was an
amazing virtuoso performance. Victor broke off – 'Now
come up here Letty.' Letty hesitated. She moved, stumbled,
and was held by Alistair.

'Up here, Letty,' Victor was implacable. Letty hesitated no
longer, but walked delicately past Melanie, Alistair and Ralph.
In the dark Melanie suspected that Alistair took the opportunity to give Letty one of his quick little hugs.

'Now I'm here just behind you.' Letty's voice came out of
the darkness. Melanie, who found she had been holding her
breath, let it out.

'Then I'll help you to pass me. You shall lead us all, Letty.'

Letty's sharp scream, long drawn out and suddenly stopped, followed by the noise of falling masonry, were the next sounds Melanie heard.

Ralph shouted: 'Hold her.' Alistair tried to pass Melanie. There was a view of Letty, hanging onto the edge of the battlements, with Victor bending over her.

'Save Letty.' It was Melanie's own voice, but at the same time Letty was somehow being helped up, and was now standing, very shakily, leaning against Victor. A moment later, Melanie registered with amazement that Victor had started to recite Othello again:

'*My wife! My wife! What wife? I have no wife . . .*' She would never be able to hear those words again, let alone go to a performance of *Othello* without dread at the memory. There was a new sound of scrabbling as Ralph tried to reassure himself that Letty was now secure. Victor stopped reciting at last.

'I'm perfectly OK now, Ralph, really. False alarm.' Letty speaking. 'I thought I was slipping, that was all. Victor saved me.' Melanie saw that Victor was holding Letty quite tightly now. They were reaching the end of the semi-circle of battlements, and he seemed to be half pushing her, half propelling her forward. The courtyard far below seemed almost as remote as the lights of Siena. Both distances were immense, downwards or away.

'I'm holding you now, Letty, aren't I?' said Victor. 'You won't slip again, will you?'

'No, no,' Letty's soft voice, breathing hard.

'Say "I won't slip again." ' There was an instant of silence. Letty was breathing so hard that Melanie for the third time in twenty-four hours, was reminded by Letty of an animal – but now it was some frightened and panting animal in distress, not a proud fox or a sly cat, but something captured and held, a runaway dog, a dog waiting to be beaten . . .

The stones on the battlements crunched and some feet moved sharply.

'I won't slip again.' Victor's voice.

'I won't slip again, Victor.' Letty's voice at last, soft, panting, frightened. It ended on a sigh. Melanie heard in it surprise, and also a kind of strange contentment. No, on the whole, she did not think Letty would slip again.

The Night Mother

There were plenty of golden windows in the big house, which stood out against the dark brick and the night sky. None of the curtains were drawn. Perhaps the people inside the windows were having too good a time to waste a moment drawing curtains. And from the top floor you could hear an occasional shout of laughter, even in the street.

'These children really must get into bed,' cried Lucy, laughing.

'And stay in bed. Once in, stay in,' added Spencer. He sounded, as usual when giving any command to the children, rather gloomy.

In any case Philip still hopped from bed to bed and Polly followed him. Lucy moved briskly to the undrawn curtains and started to twitch them across the window.

'Don't draw the curtains, Mummy Lucy,' said Polly in her most childish voice. But Lucy continued to draw.

'You spoil them, darling,' said Spencer on the way downstairs. 'Just becaue they're not your own children. You're much too soft with them.'

'I did stand firm about the curtains,' Lucy pointed out.

But Lucy's firm stand about the curtains had not had much permanent effect. Already Polly and Philip in the night nursery had drawn them back again and were peering into the darkness outside.

'Do you think she'll come tonight?' said Philip after a bit.
'She said she would.'

'It's cold and dark. Doesn't she mind that?'

'Ghosts don't mind the dark. Or the cold.' The children waited. Spencer and Lucy went out to dinner. The children watched them leave from their window. The grown-ups did not look up and thus did not observe the undrawn curtains.

A long time later the children heard the noise they were expecting: a light imperative tapping on the fire-escape window. It came from the little room next door where Inge the *au pair* girl had once slept, before Lucy's social-worker friend Rhoda came to baby-sit for them in the evenings. There was a soft scramble of children and a heavier body, then a slight thump. There was now someone in the room with them, they could feel the presence in the darkness.

'Good evening, my darlings.' The ghost, although it was clearly a woman, spoke in a low voice, much lower, for example, than Mummy Lucy's.

'Good evening, ghost,' said Philip. His voice was trembling slightly.

'Mother,' corrected the ghost. Her low voice sounded rather amused.

Polly hugged the ghost, and Philip followed suit, hugging her so fiercely even with his little arms, that the ghost gave a kind of squeak.

'You're not so cold tonight,' he said. The ghost laughed and touched his cheek.

'You're not cold either.' All three now sat on Polly's bed. The ghost lolled back and lit a cigarette.

'We've got lots more questions to ask you – ' began Polly. 'We've thought up lots more things we want to know about. It's so exciting – '

'No one else at school has two mothers,' interrupted Philip. 'We have a ghost mother and Mummy Lucy.'

'A day mother and a night mother,' said Polly. 'But we don't tell anyone about our night mother.'

'Of course we don't tell anyone,' said Philip scornfully. 'You're our own secret ghost.'

Then as usual, the ghost told them many things about her own way of life. She answered all their questions in her low and beautiful voice. She told them about hot and cold in the ghost world which was all upside down (how everything hot was cold and everything cold was hot, just as black and white and light and dark were also upside down, like the negatives in Philip's films). How Father Christmas did not live there, how Father Christmas did not in fact exist (which Polly and Phillip had long ago suspected). That on the whole it was nice being a ghost, a restful life in between hauntings, but that she missed watching her favourite television programmes, although being a ghost was rather like being inside a television screen, if she could put it like that.

The ghosts' food, too, was a promising subject. For one thing food and drink were also sort of upside down – but –

'I'll tell you about that next time,' exclaimed the ghost. She jumped up in one of those swift movements which like her voice took the children by surprise. Lucy tended to move firmly and gently when the children were around.

'Is it the cock crowing?' enquired Philip anxiously. He had begun to make seemingly casual enquiries among the grown-ups on the subjects of ghosts since the visits of the night mother had begun. He worried that the ghost might be captured by the dawn.

'Something like that.' The night mother sighed. 'It's a bit sad sometimes looking back at the house when I go, you know. The lights. So warm. Sometimes it's a bit sad being a ghost – '

'But you don't feel that once you're back with your nice ghost friends,' said Polly kindly. 'Out there where you live. Where there are no houses. It must be so exciting.'

'Did you ever live in this house, night mother?' asked Philip suddenly. 'Actually live in it?' They had never thought of asking the night mother about her past, because her present was clearly so much more interesting.

'Years ago,' said the ghost. 'But we ghosts aren't really supposed to talk about our life on earth,' she added lightly. 'It's a kind of rule. You see, it weakens us. Takes away our ghostly powers. So no more of that, my darlings.'

The ghost was through the fire-escape window and was gone. But before she went, she whispered 'I'll be back soon.'

The ghost's visits became more frequent. The ghost also began to stay later. The children began to live for her arrival. As a result they often felt quite washed out and sultry in between times, falling alseep at school, silent in answer to Lucy's kind enquiries. Lucy redoubled her maternal attentions. She took Polly to the doctor twice – those white cheeks, was there a lack of iron? – and Philip once. This was when his teacher, the conscientious Miss Carey, noticed his yawns in class and enquired – delicately – if there could be some 'home problem'?

Lucy was baffled. A home problem. Now could there be? In a way they had really been *too* happy. From the word go, Spencer's babies had been like her own, loved as her own, loving in return. Friends sometimes wondered, with delicacy equal to Miss Carey's, whether the real mother ever . . .

'Never,' Lucy would reply. 'A clean pair of heels. Imagine, two tiny children, tots they were. And Spencer just trying to build up his own business with Henry. Not a word since. Later of course Spencer made it a condition. But she never objected. Not a word.'

'Unbelievable,' said Lucy's friend Rhoda with relish. None the less she clearly had no difficulty in believing it.

'Jacintha always was completely amoral,' commented Henry's wife Pauline. 'Henry must have hated that,' observed Lucy with a serious air: she implied that there was a good deal to be said for Henry's point of view. Pauline of course had the advantage of remembering the bad old days of Spencer's first marriage. She helped herself to another drink on the strength of it, and after a convivial sip, added: 'Fascinating of course, and great fun. Quite exciting to be with in a way. She made things happen all right. But quite amoral.'

'Those sort of people are hopeless with children. Can't take responsibility,' was Rhoda's view. Although herself un-married, Rhoda worked a great deal with deprived children and was known to have achieved some wonderful results.

The doctor also used the word exciting when he gave his view of Polly and Philip's condition to Lucy: nothing organically wrong, tests showed up nothing, blood and all that sort of thing fine, fine, but they do seem to be rather excited about something.

Excited? thought Lucy. What had Polly and Philip got to be excited about? Their birthdays were both past, and it was nowhere near Christmas. All the same, conscientiously, she did her best to eliminate all possible remaining traces of excitement from their placid little round of school and home. After consultation with Rhoda, Lucy also redoubled her attentions to the children at all flashpoints of emotional security – bath-time, bedtime had become positive orgies of cuddles and stories.

It was over the latter increase that Lucy had one of her few, perhaps her only, sharp exchange with Polly. Polly, so sweet, so affectionate, so much Lucy's own little girl, became quite sulky when Lucy suggested an extra-special long read from the Green Fairy Book (long established as Polly's favourite reading).

'Oh, I just want to go to sleep, Mummy Lucy.'

'Fairies are rot anyway,' snorted Philip. But of course it had never been *his* favourite book. 'You were jolly rude to Mummy Lucy,' he told Polly afterwards, rather unfairly.

'I just didn't want her to stay, that was all. I'm so longing to see the night mother.' And Polly was extra polite and loving to Mummy Lucy all next day to make up.

Meanwhile, the night mother grew bolder still in her visitations. She laughed more. She smoked more cigarettes and was less careful about carrying the butts away with her when she departed. Her stories were wilder and funnier, and the children grew more and more excited. There was one evening when they had never laughed and shouted so much;

Philip jumping up and down on the bed, Polly clapping her hands, as the night mother told them the most absurd story in the world – or out of it – about certain inquisitive ghosts who had decided to haunt Buckingham Palace to see if the Queen wore nighties or pyjamas (yes, ghosts were still interested in that sort of thing, especially as so many of them wore garments like white nighties, indeed the whole matter had arisen because of an argument as to whether ghosts should go over to pyjamas).

'Pyjamas! A ghost in pyjamas!' Philip almost screamed with laughter.

'And which did the Queen wear?' asked Polly. But she never found out. For at that moment the door opened. The light was switched on sharply. And Spencer stood there with an expression of absolute horror, gazing at the little group which had been laughing and wriggling in the darkness, the woman and the two children.

'Jacintha!' He said it in a voice of complete disbelief.

'Spencer.' The night mother spoke with her usual half-amused calm. But Polly saw that her hands, as she lit another cigarette, were shaking. Spencer looked at the two children and without moving said in a furious voice: 'What's your mother doing in here?'

Philip was the one to speak. 'She's not our mother, she's a ghost.'

'Of course she's your mother.'

'No, Spencer, I'm a ghost, just like they said,' interrupted Jacintha.

'Jacintha, is this one of your tricks?' began Spencer, moving towards her and taking her arm rather roughly.

'I am a ghost,' she said. 'You told them I was dead. You made me into a ghost.'

'She's a ghost,' repeated Philip loudly, but he knew something was terribly wrong.

'A ghost!' shouted Spencer. 'She's no ghost. She's your mother. She left you. She ran away and left you, and all for a bloody Polish pianist – '

'Violinist,' said Jacintha in a stronger voice.

'A trumpeter for all I care. This is your mother who never wrote to you or asked about you or cared about you. She's no ghost.'

His voice must have disturbed Lucy because soon after that she too came into the room. Then there were more explanations, and some shouting. And it was Lucy who suggested very smoothly that all three grown-ups should go downstairs and have a drink. At which point it was Philip who started to scream and scream and scream, words they could hardly hear, except that the one word 'ghost, ghost, ghost' certainly kept coming into it. While Polly was silent and just put her head into the pillow. They saw her shoulders shaking as she wept, but no sound came out. In a way, as Lucy said afterwards to Spencer, Polly's reaction was really worse than Philip's. You could deal with hysterical screaming, if you were calm and loving enough, and after a bit Philip did quieten down; but Polly refused to say anything at all. Lucy had an awful fear that the silent weeping might go on all night. But at last they did both go to sleep, Philip shaking and Polly sobbing, even though both their little bodies continued to twitch and tremble long after kind oblivion had taken over.

From start to finish, it was a dreadful scene. When Jacintha had gone: 'How could anyone treat children like that? It was abominable,' Lucy kept repeating to Spencer.

'I thought children were frightened of ghosts anyway,' he replied dully after a bit. Spencer himself said over and over again: 'Jacintha! After five years without a word. Who would have thought it?' Until poor exhausted Lucy felt herself wanting to hit him.

All things considered, it was surprising how quickly everything got back to normal. For one thing, Jacintha really did show every sign of being sorry for what she had done. She apologized to both Spencer and Lucy many times. She explained to them both constantly, until they really had to see her point, about seeing the house from the outside, the lighted windows. And especially recognizing the nursery, and remembering the fire escape. About not being able to resist it, and how anyway after Stefan had left her, she had been very ill and hardly knew what she was doing –

'Bloody unreliable Pole – ' commented Spencer at this point. And somehow Jacintha had been so drawn to see the children, and get to know them, and she knew it was unusual and indeed very naughty of her to pretend to be a ghost, and she knew that Lucy had brought them up beautifully and was really their proper mother now. She would quite understand if they didn't want her to pay any more visits, real visits, but on the other hand, she did feel the children had got quite fond of her – as a ghost of course – and so if by any chance . . .

Lucy, after consultation with Rhoda, decided it would be wrong and unkind to resist such an appeal. The children's natural mother had her role to play, said Rhoda, although Lucy would of course continue to provide the centre of their emotional security. So the reformed Jacintha paid state visits at tea-times, even attended Philip's carol concert along with Lucy and Spencer, and finally went to Polly's prize giving with Spencer alone (Lucy was on holiday in Italy). She never of course returned to the roof tops, nor mentioned her previous existence as a ghost; nor did the children; nor did anyone.

Everyone agreed that the children accepted this change in their existence with wonderful calm.

'You can explain anything to children so long as their security is not disturbed,' said Rhoda triumphantly. 'All these changes centre round you, Lucy.'

'I rather thought it was Jacintha who was playing the starring role in all this.' That was Pauline, who was on her second drink, the one that brought out her bitchy streak.

And when, not really so very long after, there were still more momentous changes in Spencer's household, everyone agreed that the children took this new revolution very calmly too. It must by now have been a question of geographical security, a life always led in the same house, rather than security focused on one particular person. Because this time it was Mummy Lucy who was leaving them. Yet still the children seemed to accept this radical change with a quite remarkable philosophy, in view of the ramifications involved.

As Spencer said to Jacintha, it was complicated enough in real life, without having to explain it to two young children. He rehearsed his speech to her.

'So you see, children, Mummy Lucy wants to go off and have a baby of her own, now that you're no longer babies, and also your own Mummy, Mummy Jacintha, happens to want to come back and live with your own Daddy, Daddy Spencer. So it's really much more sensible for her to look after you with me, your Daddy that is, and Mummy Lucy to go off and have her own baby with her own Daddy, Daddy Henry, Uncle Henry that was. Because Uncle Henry like Mummy Lucy has never had any babies of his own, and as for Aunt Pauline – '

'She's too busy drinking herself into a stupor to bother one way or the other,' interrupted Jacintha, stretching out a long leg like a cat in front of the fireside which was once more hers.

'Shut up, Jacintha! I was just getting it right. So we're all going to be great friends and of course Mummy Lucy loves you just as much as she ever did, and so does Uncle, I mean Daddy, Henry (who is Philip's godfather, isn't he?) and they'll both still come to school concerts and prize days, and so will Aunt Rhoda, who is of course Polly's godmother – '

'Sanctimonious bitch,' offered Jacintha. 'Will Aunt Pauline come to concerts? That should liven them up.'

'Jacintha! I'm warning you. I must get it straight in order to break it to the children.'

But the children just smiled, and hugged Mummy Lucy goodbye when she came to collect her luggage with Uncle, now Daddy Henry, and hardly said anything. They didn't ask any questions either. So Spencer's explanation must have satisfied them. Also, they went to bed extremely cheerfully and quickly that night, to everyone's relief.

Later Polly and Philip had a thrilling conference.

'She'll come back now, won't she? The night mother.'

'The ghost you mean.'

'I think so. Mummy Lucy will be a ghost now, won't she?'

'A night mother anyway. We'll have her back. We shan't just be left with a boring old proper kind of mother.'

'It'll be secret again.'

'And exciting.'

So the children waited. They opened the latch of the fire-escape window. And they waited to see what the golden windows of the big house would attract once more out of the ghost-ridden darkness.

Who's Been Sitting In My Car?

'Who's been sitting in my car?' said Jacobine. She said it in a stern gruff voice, like a bear. In fact Jacobine looked more like a Scottish Goldilocks with her pale fair hair pulled back from her round forehead. The style betokened haste and worry, the worry of a girl late for school. But it was Jacobine's children who were late, and she was supposed to be driving them.

'Someone's been smoking in my car,' Jacobine added, pointing to the ash-tray crammed with butts.

'Someone's been driving your car, you mean.' It was Gavin, contradictory as usual. 'People don't just sit in cars. They drive them.' He elaborated. 'Someone's been driving my car, said the little bear – '

'People do sit in cars. We're sitting in a car now.' Tessa, because she was twelve months older, could never let that sort of remark from Gavin pass.

'Be quiet, darlings,' said Jacobine automatically. She continued to sit looking at the ash-tray in front of her. It certainly looked quite horrible with all its mess of ash and brown stubs. And there was a sort of violence about the way it had been stuffed: you wondered that the smoker had not bothered to throw at least a few of them out of the window.

Instead he had remorselessly gone on pressing them into the little chromium tray, hard, harder, into the stale pyre.

Jacobine did not smoke. Rory, her ex-husband, had been a heavy smoker. And for one moment she supposed that Rory might have used an old key to get into the Mini, and then sat endlessly smoking outside the house . . . It was a mad thought and almost instantly Jacobine recognized it as such. For one thing she had bought the Mini second-hand after the divorce. Since ferrying the children had become her main activity these days, she had spent a little money on making it as convenient as possible. More to the point, Jacobine and Rory were on perfectly good terms; both still lived in Edinburgh as they had done when they were married to each other.

'Married too young,' was the general verdict. Jacobine agreed. She still felt rather too young for marriage, as a matter of fact: in an upside down sort of way, two children seemed to be all she could cope with. She really quite liked Rory's new wife, Fiona, for her evident competence in dealing with the problem of living with him.

It was only that the mucky filled ash-tray had reminded Jacobine of the household details of life with Rory. But if not Rory, who? And why did she feel, on top of disgust, a very strong sensation of physical fear? Jacobine, habitually timid, did not remember feeling fear before in quite such an alarmingly physical manner. Her terrors were generally projections into the future, possible worries concerned with the children. Jacobine was suddenly convinced that the smoker had an ugly streak of cruelty in his nature – as well as being of course a potential thief. She had a nasty new image of him sitting there in her car outside her house. Waiting for her. Watching the house. She dismissed it.

'Tessa, Gavin, stay where you are.' Jacobine jumped out of the driver's seat and examined the locks of the car. Untouched, both of them.

'Mummy, we are going to be late,' whined Tessa. That decided Jacobine. Back to the car, key in lock and away. They had reached the corner of Melville Street when the next odd thing happened. The engine died and the little Mini gradually and rather feebly came to a halt.

'No petrol!' shouted Gavin from the back.

'Oh darling, do be quiet,' began Jacobine. When her eye fell on the gauge. He was right. The Mini was out of petrol. Jacobine felt completely jolted as if she had been hit in the face. It was as uncharacteristic of her carefully ordered existence to run out of petrol as for example to run out of milk for the children's breakfast – a thing which had happened once and still gave Jacobine shivers of self-reproach. In any case, another unpleasantly dawning realization: she had only filled up two days ago . . .

'Someone's definitely been driving this car,' she exclaimed before she could stop herself.

'That's what I said!' crowed Gavin, 'Someone's been driving my car, said the little bear.'

'Oh Mummy, we are going to be awfully late,' pleaded Tessa. 'Miss Hamilton doesn't like us being late. She says Mummies should be more thoughtful.'

The best thing to do was to take them both to school in a taxi and sort out the car's problems later. One way and another, it was lunch-time before Jacobine was able to consider the intruding driver again. And then, sturdily, she dismissed the thought. So that, curiously enough, finding the Mini once more empty of petrol and the ash-tray packed with stubs the following morning, was even more of a shock. Nor was it possible to escape the sharp eyes of the children, or gloss over the significance of the rapid visit to the petrol station. In any case, Tessa had been agonizing on the subject of lateness due to petrol failure since breakfast.

'I shall go to the police,' said Jacobine firmly. She said it as much to reassure herself as to shut up the children. In fact the visit was more irritating than reassuring. Although Jacobine began her complaint with the statement that she had locked the car, and the lock had not been tampered with, she was left with the strong impression that the police did not believe any part of her story. They did not seem to accept either that the doors had been locked or that the petrol was missing, let alone appreciate the significance of the used ash-tray. All the same, they viewed her tale quite indulgently, and were positively gallant when Jacobine revealed that she lived, as they put it, 'with no man to look after you'.

'Of course you worry about the car, madam, it's natural. I expect your husband did all that when you were married,' said the man behind the broad desk. 'Tell you what, I know where you live, I'll tell the policeman on the beat to keep a special watch on it, shall I? Set your mind at rest. That's what we're here for. Prevention is better than cure.'

Jacobine trailed doubtfully out of the station. Prevention is better than cure. It was this parting homily which gave her the inspiration to park the Mini for the night directly under the street-light, which again lay under the children's window. If the police did not altogether believe her, she did not altogether believe them in their kindly promises. Anyway, the light would make their task easier, if they did choose to patrol the tree-shaded square.

That evening Jacobine paid an unusually large number of visits to the children's room after they went to sleep. Each time she looked cautiously out of the window. The Mini, small and green, looked like a prize car at the motor show, in its new spotlight. You could hardly believe it had an engine inside it. It might have been a newly painted dummy. The shock of seeing the Mini gone on her fifth visit of inspection was therefore enormous. At the same time, Jacobine did feel a tiny pang of satisfaction. Now let the police treat her as an hysterical female, she thought, as she dialled 999 with slightly shaking fingers. Her lips trembled too as she dictated the number of the car: 'AST 5690. A bright green Mini. Stolen not more than ten minutes ago. I warned you it might happen.'

'Don't worry, madam, we'll put out a general call for it.' Why did everyone tell her not to worry?

'No, it's my car, not my husband's,' she told him. 'I haven't got a husband.'

Jacobine tried to sleep after that, but her mind raced, half in rage at the impudence of the intruder, half in imagined triumph that he would be hauled before her, cigarette hanging from his lips, those tell-tale polluting cigarettes . . . It was the door-bell weaving in and out of these hazy dreams which finally ended them. At first she assumed they were bringing round the thief, even at this time of night.

It was a policeman, a new one from the morning's encounter. But he was alone.

'Mrs Esk? Sorry to call so late. About your stolen Mini – '

'Have you found it? Who took it?'

'Well, that's the point, madam. A green Mini, registration number AST 5690, reported stolen twenty minutes ago at Ferry Road police station, is now outside your door.'

Jacobine stared. It was true. The Mini was back.

'He must have known you were looking for him.' She blurted out the remark and then regretted it. Silently, Jacobine in her quilted dressing-gown and slippers, and the policeman in his thick night-black uniform examined the Mini from every angle. The locks were pristine, and the car itself was locked. They examined the dashboard. It was untouched.

'Perhaps there was some mistake?' suggested the policeman in the gentle tone Jacobine had come to associate with his colleagues. 'You only looked out of the window, you said. In the lamplight, you know . . . Well, I'd better be getting back to the station and report that all is well. You don't want to be arrested for driving your own Mini tomorrow, do you?' He sounded quite paternal.

'Look, he only had time for two cigarettes,' said Jacobine suddenly. At least she had curtailed the nocturnal pleasures of her adversary. On the other hand there was a new and rather horrible development. The car positively *smelt*. It did. She did not like to point that out to the policeman, since he had not mentioned it. Perhaps he was embarrassed. It was a strong, pungent, human smell which had nothing to do with Jacobine or the children or even cigarettes. As Jacobine had envisaged someone cruel and even violent when she first saw the ash-tray, she now conjured up involuntarily someone coarse and even brutal.

Jacobine had not thought much about sex since the end of her marriage. Now she found herself thinking of it, in spite of herself. It was the unmistakable animal smell of sex which overpoweringly filled her nostrils.

The next night Jacobine put the children to bed early. Still fully dressed, with a large new torch beside her, she took up her vigil in the lobby next to the front door. A little after eleven o'clock, with apprehension but also with excitement, she heard the noise of an engine running. It was close to the house. It was the peculiar coughing start of her own car.

Without considering what she was doing, Jacobine flung open the front door, ran towards the kerb and shouted: 'Stop it, stop it, stop thief!' The engine stopped running instantly. It was as though it had been cut short in mid-sentence. Jacobine wrenched at the passenger door, her fingers trembling so much that she fumbled with the familiar handle. It did not open. Even locked against her: her own car! In her passion, Jacobine rapped hard on the window.

Nothing happened. Very slowly, Jacobine realized that the driver's seat, and indeed the whole of the tiny car, was empty. In the ash-tray, illuminated by the street-lamp like a detail in a moonlit picture, lay one cigarette, still alight. Jacobine was now suddenly aware of her thumping heart as the anger which had driven her on drained away. For the first time she had no idea what to do. After a pause, during which she stood gazing at the locked Mini and the gradually disintegrating cigarette, she walked back into the house. She picked up the car keys. Even more slowly, she returned to the car and unlocked it. Deliberately, but very gingerly, she climbed into the front seat and touched the cigarette. Yes, warm. The car smelt fearfully.

'Sweetheart,' said a voice very close to her ear. 'You shouldn't have told the police, you know. You shouldn't have done that. You have to be punished for that, don't you?'

Jacobine felt herself grasped roughly and horribly. What happened next was so unexpected in its outrageous nature, that she tried to scream out her revulsion. But at the same time a pair of lips, thick hard rubbery lips, pressed on to her own. The car was still to her staring frantic eyes above her muted mouth, palpably empty.

'Oh God, I've been taken,' she thought, as she choked and struggled.

'But you like it, don't you, Sweetheart?' as though she had managed to speak aloud. It was not true.

'I'm going to be sick, I think,' said Jacobine. This time she did manage to say it out loud.

'But you'll come back for more tomorrow night, won't you, Sweetheart,' said the voice. 'And we'll go for a drive together.' She was released. Jacobine fumbled with the door once more and half-retching, fled towards the house.

She did not dare leave it again that night but lay in her bed, trembling and shaking. Even a bath did not help to wash away her body's memories of the assault. The next morning, as soon as the children were at school, Jacobine went to the police station. From the start, the man behind the desk was rather more wary of her, she thought. He listened to her new story with rather a different expression, no less kind, but somewhat more speculative. At the end, without commenting on Jacobine's nocturnal experience, he asked her abruptly if she had ever seen a doctor since the break-up of her marriage.

'I need the police, not a doctor, for something like this,' said Jacobine desperately. 'I need protection.'

'I'm not quite so sure, Mrs Esk,' said the policeman. 'Now look here, why don't you have a word first of all with your GP? It's not very pleasant being a woman on your own, is it, and maybe a few pills, a few tranquillizers . . .'

When Jacobine left the station, it was with a sinking feeling that he had not believed her at all. The rest of the day, she agonized over what to do. Ring Rory? That was ridiculous. But Jacobine had no other figure of authority in her life. A lawyer might help, she thought vaguely, remembering the sweet young man who had helped her over the divorce. Yet even a lawyer would ask for more proof, if the police had proved so sceptical. With dread, Jacobine realized that it was up to her to provide it.

About eleven o'clock that night, therefore, she took up her position in the driver's seat. She was not quite sure what to expect, except that there would be a moment's wait while she settled herself.

'I'm glad you're early, Sweetheart,' said the voice conversationally. 'Because we'll be able to go for a really long drive. We've got so much to talk about, haven't we? The children, for example. I don't really like your children. You'll have to get rid of them, you know.'

'Don't you dare touch my chidren,' gasped Jacobine.

'Oh rather you than me,' said the voice. 'My methods aren't as pretty as yours. A car crash on the way to school, for example, which would leave you uninjured . . .'

Jacobine gave a little sick cry. She envisaged those precious tended bodies . . . the recurring nightmare of motherhood.

'I know all about crashes and children, their precious bodies,' went on the voice. He seemed to read her thoughts, her ghastly images. 'Poor little mangled things.'

Jacobine could no longer bear it. The smell combined with terror overwhelmed her. And the police station was so near. Jumping out of the car, abandoning her persecutor, she ran along the road in the general direction of the station. A few minutes later she heard the engine start up. The car was following her. Her heart banged in her chest. She had time to think that it was more frightening being pursued by a car, an empty car, than by anything in the world, human and alive, when she gained the safety of the steps. The car stopped, neatly, and remained still.

'He's threatening the children now. He says he's going to kill them,' Jacobine began her story. It seemed that she had hardly gulped it out before a policewoman was taking her back – on foot – to her house. The policewoman concentrated on the fact that Jacobine had left her children alone in the house while she went out to the car. Indeed, although it had not occurred to Jacobine at the time, it was very much outside her usual character. The car was driven back by a policeman. It looked very chic and small and harmless when it came to rest once more outside Jacobine's front door.

It was two days later that Rory rang up. In between Jacobine had not dared to leave the intruder alone in the car at night in case he carried out his threat against the children during the day. On Saturday he performed the same act of possession which had initiated their relationship. On Sunday he brought up the subject of the children again. First he made Jacobine drive as far as Arthur's Seat, then round through silent Edinburgh. Jacobine was tired when she got back, and the Mini was allowed to park beside her house once more. A policeman noted her sitting there, a smouldering cigarette propped above the dashboard, and he heard her cry out. In answer to his questions, she would only point to the cigarette. She was wearing, he saw, a nightdress under her coat. At the time, the policeman was not quite sure whether Jacobine was crying out in terror or delight.

Actually what had forced that strange hoarse sound out of Jacobine was neither fear nor pleasure. It was, in its weird way, a sort of cry of discovery, a confirmation of a dread, but also bringing relief from the unknown.

She had got to know, perforce, the voice a little better during their long night drive. It was some chance remark of his about the car, some piece of mechanical knowledge, which gave her the clue. Proceeding warily – because the voice could often, but not always, read her thoughts – Jacobine followed up her suspicions. In any case, she preferred talking about the car to listening to the voice on the subject of her children. She tried to shut her mind to his gibes and sometimes quite surprisingly petty digs against Tessa and Gavin. He seemed to be out to belittle the children as well as eliminate them from Jacobine's life.

'Fancy Gavin not being able to read – at seven,' he would say. 'I heard him stumbling over the smallest words the other day. What a baby!' And again: 'Tessa makes an awful fuss about being punctual for one so young, doesn't she? I can just see her when she grows up. A proper little spinster. If she grows up, that is . . .'

Jacobine interrupted this by wondering aloud how she had got such a bargain in the shape of a second-hand Mini which had hardly done a thousand miles.

'Oh yes, Sweetheart,' exclaimed the voice. 'You certainly did get a bargain when you bought this car. All things considered. It had always been very well looked after, I can tell you – '

'Then it was your car!' Jacobine tried to stop her own voice shaking as she burst out with her discovery. 'This was your car once, wasn't it?'

'There was an accident,' replied the voice. He spoke in quite a different tone, she noticed: dully, flatly, nothing like his usual accents which varied from a horrid predatory kind of lustfulness to the near-frenzy of his dislike for the children.

'Tell me.'

'It was her children. On the way to school. There was an accident.' It was still quite a different tone, so much so that Jacobine almost thought – it was a ridiculous word to use under the circumstances – that he sounded quite human. The smell in the car lessened and even the grip which he habitually kept on her knee, that odious grip, seemed to become softer, more beseeching than possessing.

'She worked so hard. She always had so many things to do for them. I was just trying to help her, taking them to school for her. It was an accident. A mistake. Otherwise why didn't I save myself? An accident, I tell you. And she won't forgive me. Oh why won't she forgive me? I can't rest till she forgives me.' It was piteous now and Jacobine heard a harsh, racking sobbing, a man's sobbing which hurts the listener. She yielded to some strange new impulse and put out her left hand tentatively towards the passenger seat. The next moment she was grasped again, more firmly than before, the assault began again, the smell intensified.

'I've got you now, Sweetheart, haven't I?' said the voice. 'It doesn't matter about her any more. Let her curse me all she likes. We've got each other. Once we get rid of your children, that is. And I'm awfully good at getting rid of children.'

When Rory rang up on Monday he was uneasy and embarrassed.

'It's all so unlike Jacobine,' he complained to Fiona. 'She's really not the type. And you should have heard some of the things she told the policeman this fellow in the car had done to her.'

'Oh those quiet types,' exclaimed Fiona. Without knowing Jacobine intimately, she had always thought it odd that she should have surrendered such an attractive man as Rory, virtually without a struggle. 'Still waters,' Fiona added brightly.

Rory suggested a visit to the doctor. He also wondered whether the strain of running a car . . . Jacobine felt the tears coming into her eyes. Why hadn't she thought of that? Get rid of him. Get rid of the car. Free herself.

'Oh Rory,' she begged. 'Would you take Tessa and Gavin for a few days. I know it's not your time, and I appreciate that Fiona's job – '

'I'll have them at the weekend,' suggested Rory, always as placating as possible, out of guilt that Jacobine, unlike him, had not married again. 'Fiona's got a marketing conference this week and I'll be in Aberdeen.'

'No, please, Rory, today, I implore you. I tell you what, I'll send them round in a taxi. I won't come too. I'll just put them in a taxi this afternoon.'

But Rory was adamant. It would have to be the weekend.

That afternoon, picking up Tessa and Gavin from school, Jacobine very nearly hit an old woman on a zebra crossing. She had simply not seen her. She could not understand it. She always slowed down before zebra crossings and yet she had been almost speeding across this one. Both children bumped themselves badly and Gavin in the front seat, who was not wearing his safety belt (another odd factor, since Jacobine could have sworn she fastened it herself) cut himself on the driving mirror.

'That's your warning,' he said that night. 'The children must go. You spend too much time thinking about them and bothering about them. Tiresome little creatures. I'm glad they hurt themselves this afternoon. Cry babies, both of them. Besides, I don't want you having any other calls on your time.'

And Jacobine was wrenched very violently to and fro, shaken like a shopping bag. The next moment was worse. A cigarette was stubbed, hard, on her wrist, just where the veins ran.

Even at the instant of torture, Jacobine thought: 'Now they'll have to believe me.'

But it seemed that they didn't. In spite of the mark and in spite of the fact that surely everyone knew Jacobine did not smoke. A doctor came. And Rory came. Jacobine got her wish in the sense that Tessa and Gavin were taken away by Rory. Fiona had to break off half-way through her marketing conference, although you would never have guessed it from the cheery way she saluted the children.

'Just because their mother's gone nuts,' Fiona said sensibly to Rory afterwards, 'it doesn't mean that I can't give them a jolly good tea. And supper too. I have no idea what happened about their meals with all that jazzing about at night, and running around in her nightie, and screaming.'

Then Rory took Jacobine down to a really pleasant countrified place not far from Edinburgh, recommended by the doctor. It had to be Rory: there was no one else to do it. Jacobine was very quiet all the way down. Rory wondered whether it was because he was driving her car – the car. But Fiona needed the Cortina to fetch the children from school. Once or twice he almost thought Jacobine was listening to something in her own head. It gave him a creepy feeling. Rory put on the radio.

'Don't do that,' said Jacobine, quite sharply for her. 'He doesn't like it.' Rory thought it prudent to say nothing. But he made a mental note to report back to Fiona when he got home. For it was Fiona who felt some concern about despatching Jacobine in this way.

'It's really rather awful, darling,' she argued. 'Taking her children away from her. They're all she had in her life. Poor dotty girl.'

'They are my children too,' said Rory humbly. But he knew just what Fiona meant. He admired her more than ever for being so resolutely kind hearted: it was wonderful how well she got on with both Tessa and Gavin as a result. Fiona also took her turn visiting Jacobine when Rory was too busy. There were really no limits to her practical good nature. And so it was Fiona who brought back the news.

'She wants the car.'

'The car!' cried Rory. 'I should have thought that was the very last thing she should have under the circumstances.'

'Not to drive. She doesn't even want the keys. Just the car. She says she likes the idea of sitting in it. It makes her feel safe to know the car's there and not free to go about wherever it likes. I promise you, those were her very words.'

'What did Doctor Mackie say? It seems very rum to me.'

'Oh, he seemed quite airy about it. Talked about womb transference – can that be right – anyway that sort of thing. He said it could stay in the grounds. Like a sort of Wendy House, I suppose. She hasn't been making very good progress. She cries so much, you see. It's pathetic. Poor thing, let her have the car. She has so little,' ended Fiona generously.

So Jacobine got her car back. Doctor Mackie had it parked as promised in a secluded corner of the gardens. He was encouraged to find that Jacobine cried much less now. She spent a great deal of time sitting alone in the driver's seat, talking to herself; she was clearly happier.

'It's much better like this,' said the voice. 'I'm glad we got rid of your children the *nice* way. You won't ever see them again you know.' Jacobine did not answer. She was getting quite practised at pleasing him. He was generally waiting for her when she arrived at the Mini in its shady corner.

'Who's been sitting in my car?' she would say in a mock-gruff voice, pointing to the heap of butts in the ash-tray. But in spite of everything Jacobine still looked more like Goldilocks than a bear. Indeed, her face had come to look even younger since she lost the responsibility of the children – or so Fiona told Rory.

Jacobine had to be specially charming on the days when Fiona came down to see her, in case He got into her car and went back to find the children after all. She thought about them all the time. But she no longer cried in front of Him. Because that made Him angry and then He would leave her. She had to keep Him sitting beside her. That way the children would be safe. From Him.

blog and newsletter

For literary discussion, author insight,
book news, exclusive content,
recipes and giveaways, visit the
Weidenfeld & Nicolson blog and
sign up for the newsletter at:

www.wnblog.co.uk

For breaking news, reviews and exclusive competitions
Follow us 🐦 @wnbooks
Find us 📘 facebook.com/WNfiction